Carol:
I hope you find
it worth the
wait!

Susan M. Hooper

Dec. 2004

Murder Junction

by

Susan M. Hooper

authorHOUSE™

1663 LIBERTY DRIVE, SUITE 200
BLOOMINGTON, INDIANA 47403
(800) 839-8640
WWW.AUTHORHOUSE.COM

First published by AuthorHouse 10/27/04

ISBN: 1-4184-8788-0 (sc)

Printed in the United States of America
Bloomington, Indiana

This book is printed on acid-free paper.

Other books by this author:

Belle Harbor Skeletons

A Barnaby Moss/Arnie Kotkin Mystery

Dedication

This book is dedicated to my father, Bill Hooper, who is also my proudest audience, and my sisters, Joanne and Maureen, who have always stood by me.

I owe a special debt of gratitude to my sister, Maureen, who paid shipping.

Preface

In 2000, I began to work on a character study involving parental reactions to the news that a grown son was gay; it turned into my first novel, ***Belle Harbor Skeletons.***

Not long after completing the original manuscript, I found that it was necessary to re-visit Belle Harbor to find out exactly how the characters had dealt with the aftermath of the events they had 'lived' through. Arnie, in particular, had not done as well as I originally believed.

In Maple Grove Junction, Vermont, a town so dull even its own residents consider watching the staff at the local cinema make popcorn to be entertaining, Arnie and Barnaby think they have found a restful spot for their vacation, until a guest at the same inn loses her head…literally.

Introduction

Barnaby Moss and Arnie Kotkin have been friends since their boyhood days of schoolyard squabbles and choirboy impersonations. After graduating from college, each of them realized that they were more than friends.

Domestic partners for over a year now, they have struggled to get through events that would have torn many couples apart—everything from attempted murder to the real thing.

Taking what should have been an enjoyable trip to Vermont in October, they find that red is not only the color of the leaves on the trees…it is also the color of blood on the ground.

Chapter 1

Attorney Jamison Hart, a red-faced, balding mountain of a man, looked across his massive oak desk at an assistant he considered small potatoes, and drummed his short, thick fingers impatiently. In just over three weeks, one of the biggest real estate deals he had ever taken a crack at would slip through those same fat fingers.

As a practical point, the aging lawyer knew the person seated across from him stood almost no chance of success; far more experienced people in his office had already failed.

Hart was willing to listen to his assistant's proposition on the outside chance that there might be something to it, but he really did not expect much…but then again, David had slain Goliath.

Making the claim, "I know I can do this," the assistant's voice oozed smug self-confidence.

Hart exploded, "Better people than you have failed to get that property. What makes you so cock sure you can do it?" With steely eyes and a hardened mouth, Hart studied his younger colleague for several seconds, and then said, "The whole deal hinges on getting that land. If we can't get the entire parcel for Yantzing by the end of the month, the deal's off."

"I understand that, Mr. Hart," the assistant said calmly. "Yantzing wants the extra land in its back pocket now, for expansion later."

"That's exactly right," Hart boomed. "They don't want to be locked into just the acreage from the biggest lot, even though it's big enough to float the mall right now. This thing's gonna grow, and grow fast…being right off I-91, how can it miss?" He pounded his mammoth fist sharply on the desk to punctuate his sentence.

"It can't" Hart's cohort said, totally undaunted by his gruff manner. "I've seen the traffic flow charts. I-91 is one of the busiest highways in New England. 'Vermont Country Estates Mall' has the potential to be the biggest thing to hit that area in years…it'll put Maple Grove Junction on the map…"

"Only if we can get the entire parcel" Hart interrupted, throwing his hands up in the air. He could not believe that his firm was blowing this, but already he had heard jokes that Hart & Associates had snatched defeat from the jaws of victory.

"Mr. Hart, I told you I could handle this. I've got some information that will change things..."

Jamison Hart cut in quickly. "What kind of information?" he demanded.

"It's a long story...difficult to explain..."

"Explain it...we've got all night," the senior partner barked.

Smirking at his underling, he added, "If it's good enough, I may send one of my other people up there. So far, they've done nothing but waste postage, and run up the office phone bill. One of 'em ought to be able to do the job they're getting paid for."

"I have to do this, Mr. Hart." The associate sneered back at the senior partner, and in a condescending voice stated, "In all due respect to my colleagues, I think I'm the only one who can pull it off...it's my plan, after all."

Hart crossed his trunk-like arms across the wide expanse of his chest, and listened...and listened...and listened.

When his associate finally finished speaking, a long-buried sense of decency made Hart say, "We can't do that...it's extortion, or at least fraud; you know it as well as I do."

The assistant smiled evilly, and said, "You don't care about that any more than I do. Neither one of us has any scruples,

3

Mr. Hart. Besides, who'd the old hag hire that you couldn't buy off? Daniel Webster died a long time ago."

Years earlier, Hart would have fought his position a lot harder, but ideology had died out quickly in the attorney; the world was cruel, and he had learned to give back as good as he got. Decency did not put food on his table, fancy clothes on his young wife's body, or pay alimony to his first two wives.

These days, for the right price, Jamison Hart would have sold his own soul…most people thought he already had.

"Go ahead" he said, "but you're on your own…I haven't authorized this."

Chapter 2

Sunset painted the autumn sky with broad brushstrokes of magenta, splashed with iridescent gold.

Casually clad in faded jeans, with a heavy, green cardigan sweater covering his newest Springstein T-shirt, and sneakers covering his feet of lead, Barnaby Moss blazed up I-91N.

"Look at that sky, would ya'?" he said to his nervous front seat passenger.

"Look at that car in front of us, would ya'?" Arnie Kotkin answered. "I'd really like for us not to end up in its trunk."

Accustomed to the passenger seat jitters of his friend, Barn grinned and replied, "Relax, I'm watching the road, Arnie, but the sky's right in front of me. How can I miss it?" Even as he spoke, the young driver's eyes remained on the road.

Arnie bit back his response; there was no point in saying 'Just miss the car, Barn'. He tugged sharply on the zipper of his leather jacket, as though he was zipping his full lips.

The seemingly insignificant gesture was not wasted on Barn's peripheral vision; he smirked silently at the body language. With his eyes still intently on the road, he asked, "How's the baby? Did your mother call last night?"

The baby in question was Arnie's nephew, Todd, the illegitimate offspring of his late brother, Jerry. Todd lived with his maternal grandparents; his mother was in jail—Jerry had always known how to pick interesting girlfriends.

Slapping his corduroy covered thigh, Arnie answered, "God, I completely forgot! Mom called me late yesterday afternoon…you were still at the studio."

Remembering how quickly they had eaten last night so they could start packing, the man in the passenger seat grinned slyly, also recalling that packing was not all they had done after supper.

"We got busy with other things after we finished packing last night" he began, "and it slipped my mind."

Barn returned his partner's devious grin, and admitted, "We spent quite a bit more time on 'other things' than on packing, as I recall." Speeding up to pass the car ahead of them, he asked, "So, did she have any news?"

Arnie answered, "Yes. She said Todd's gonna be spending Thanksgiving week with her and Pop...they're both pretty excited about it."

"That's great!" Barn enthused. "Is he walking yet?" he immediately asked, trying to form a mental picture of Arnie's parents chasing a toddler around their Pennsylvania farmhouse.

"No, but he's almost the same age as Emily, and she's really working at it..."

Barn interrupted with another thought, asking, "Are her parents still taking him to the jail to see his mother?"

"Yes," Arnie answered matter-of-factly. "He knows she's 'Mama'...he has no idea where they're going right now." After a moment's reflection, he added, "It's gonna be hard on him once he's in school; little kids can be vicious. All of his grandparents want him to know that she's really not a monster."

Barn glanced over at his friend, surprised by his last remark, yet understanding it completely. "Despite what she did, your parents feel sorry for her," he observed.

Arnie scratched his head thoughtfully. "They do, and they don't," he finally said. "It's probably the same way I feel about Jim…" His voice trailed off.

After traveling a few minutes in silence, Barn intruded on his partner's thoughts, saying, "I know I've mentioned this before, but it really was good of your parents to arrange to have Jerry's share of the trust fund released for child support…essentially, that's what he got killed for."

"It is ironic," Arnie said.

Even now it was hard to believe that Jerry's former lover had forced his car off the highway so that, in death, she could get from him the child support he had refused to give her in life.

"It was the right thing to do, though…I've always thought so," Barn said.

"Yes, it was…Todd's their grandchild" Arnie said, soberly. "The trust was written badly," he went on. "I can't imagine why a grandfather would set up a trust fund for three grandsons, but never consider the possibility that one of 'em might not make it to 25, but still leave a child."

"It was shortsighted," Barn agreed. "I'm surprised his attorneys didn't call it to his attention…although maybe they did, and he just didn't listen."

Arms crossed, Arnie looked silently out the window at the darkening autumn landscape. He finally said, "I have a feeling that my grandfather didn't listen to too many people." More quietly, he added, "Mom wasted a lot of years emulating him."

"She's really changed her act a lot," Barn said. "I give her credit for that. It can't have been easy."

"No, but it was time," Arnie replied. "It took a lot, but she finally woke up."

"Yeah…finally" Barn agreed, before changing the subject. "Temporary insanity really looked like a good shot—for Jerry's girlfriend I mean."

"I wondered how that was gonna help Mom," Arnie grinned.

His partner continued with a smile, "It could help your father, but let's not go there."

Growing serious again, Barn explained, "What I wanted to say was that I actually thought she might get off…she was a very sympathetic figure."

Arnie recalled his brother's killer sobbing in court, sometimes uncontrollably, throughout her three-week trial.

Ignoring the stab of pain his own words caused him, he stated truthfully, "I think we all thought that at one time or another; Jerry was rotten to her. The defense didn't go that far overboard in saying he contributed to his own demise."

The partners fell into a silence that lasted for the final 15 miles of their trip; they each had a lot of thinking to do.

> <

The two young men in the front seat of the northbound red Toyota had been friends since childhood, and domestic partners for the last 18 months. They were traveling to Vermont, where they would be united in a same-sex civil union on Wednesday of the upcoming week.

So far, their life together had included Barn being shot in an attempted murder, an actual murder, and more than one other surprise—not the least of which was the revelation that Arnie was a branch on a slightly different family tree than the one he had always believed—and those events had taken a far greater toll on each of the partners than either of them admitted for a long time.

Psychologically, Arnie had suffered the most.

The young post-grad student was facing more emotional turmoil than he could possibly handle—and he was piling schoolwork on top of it. Even as he presented a face that said he was fine, Arnie wondered how long it would take before he cracked.

Least inconsequential to him were his feelings about his brothers-turned-cousins, James and Jerrold Kotkin.

Some days he hated both of them, and other days he grieved for both of them...but most days it was a few hours of each.

Jim, his conceited older brother, was once a medical student with a brilliant future ahead of him. Following his role in the shooting of Barnaby Moss, and his own subsequent mental breakdown, Jim had been confined to an institution.

Arnie, to his own private shame, could not make himself visit his brother—even feeling that Jim was driven to his crime by a vicious betrayal, he still hated him for what he had done. At the same time, he found himself grieving for the loss of the life Jim could have lived.

It was a torturous cycle of emotional upheaval.

Jerry, his younger brother, had been an arrogant, rude, self-centered and completely irresponsible young man. A master of the dubious skills of deception and denial, he had imposed his own death sentence by denying paternity of the child his former lover carried.

While Arnie recognized those facts, and fully believed they earned his younger brother a free ticket to an early grave, he was still plagued by the memory of an infant he had looked at with adoring eyes just over 20 years ago—a little bundle of wrinkly pink skin and fuzzy golden hair, who was entrusted to him by his father with the tender words, "Arnie, this is Jerry. You have to take care of him, son. He's your baby brother."

Sometimes, the memories of Jerry's life were more painful for Arnie to remember than the memories of his death.

Benjamin Fentnor, Arnie's natural brother, died barely an hour after his birth. Arnie was just a small child then—little more than a toddler—and he had already been adopted by Thelma and Joseph Kotkin, the sister and brother-in-law of his natural mother.

Arnie had another sibling now—a very young one. Emily Kathryn Fentnor was born when her mother was 40 and her father was 43.

The Fentnors had spent all of their married life treasuring whatever time they were allowed to have with their first son, grieving the loss of their second one, and praying for a third child; now they had her, and she would be the joy of their middle years.

With her mother's fair skin and hazel eyes, and her father's dark, wavy hair, the 11-month-old Emily resembled a chubby, porcelain doll as she traveled from room to room, crawling when she had to, and pulling herself to her feet for tentative steps whenever she could. So far, the precious baby girl with the pretty ringlet curls crashed more than she walked, but it would not be long before she ran.

Arnie's natural mother, Helene Fine, had been only 16 years old when he was born—15 when she had conceived him. Her family had hustled her away to a so-called finishing school in upstate New York before she could even tell his teenaged father about his expected arrival.

Jack Fentnor, the young father in question, had turned 19 by the time his son entered the world completely unbeknownst to him.

After having no contact with each other since the night of Arnie's conception, the one-time lovers began to date seriously when Jack was 22 and Helene was 19, and her boorish, self-important family could no longer interfere with her life.

On the night Jack proposed, he and Helene had taken her adorable young nephew with them to McDonald's, and he was sitting next to her, stuffing a cheeseburger into his fat little face, when Jack popped the question.

Before answering, Helene had finally told Jack the truth— her darling, golden-haired 'nephew' was their son.

While he would never have admitted it to them, there had been many days when Arnie was troubled by thoughts of his humble beginnings on a lovers' lane in Belle Harbor… it was embarrassing to realize that he was the unintentional product of a first-time sexual encounter between two teenagers, and not the much-wanted child of a married couple.

Arnie's most constant inner turmoil stemmed from his personal feelings toward his legal parents; he loved them, but he did not like what they had done.

He believed he should have known he was adopted—and who his natural parents were—way before the 24th year of his life, if only to spare him the tremendous shock that came later.

Arnie fervently believed that Thelma Kotkin's most compelling reason for nearly a quarter century of silence was to spare herself from being embarrassed. To her, Helene's high school pregnancy was on par with the world's worst crime...what would people think? It still hurt to know that his mother had put her feelings before his own.

Joseph Kotkin, the Casper Milquetoast of Belle Harbor, had been against the deception—just as he had been against certain other things—but he had never been man enough to stop any of it, even knowing that when his middle son did learn the truth he would be shocked beyond words.

Family tribulations were not the youthful post-grad student's only lingering problems. Now working toward his doctorate in science, Arnie still raged inwardly whenever he recalled his brief suspension, hasty reinstatement and eventual resignation from his teaching position last year.

Amidst the media furor surrounding Barn's shooting, Arnie's character had been called into question when the mother of a student in his class apparently attempted to help him by stating that he had a good rapport with children.

Unfortunately, she chose to make her remark to the same newspaper that disclosed their relationship to the public, and for several days the story continued to appear in various papers.

Even if he read about it in that particular day's edition of the paper, Arnie had always been surprised by the number of calls on his answering machine at night.

Whether or not Arnie was gay had no bearing on whether or not he could teach science, and the Board had quickly rectified its decision, and reinstated him. He had been back on the job technically—if not physically—on the day he had brought his partner home from the hospital; however, Howard Tucker, the science department Head, made ridding the school of the young science teacher his goal.

Ultimately, Arnie tendered his resignation of his own free will—but it still rankled him.

Barn did not escape unscathed either, although with his incredible sense of humor, and deep-rooted belief that he could do anything he set his mind to, he really had done well for several months.

For the most part, what Barnaby Moss lacked in height, he compensated for in guts.

Surviving a shooting that had the potential to leave him paralyzed, the plucky recording engineer failed to make the full recovery his surgeon had optimistically predicted.

Ultimately, growing frustration stemming from that failure had been his undoing.

Barn would have been highly insulted to hear himself referred to as a 'dial jockey', but the truth of it was that he did ride a dial all day long, and after about only two hours at the consol, his left arm was numb from his shoulder all the way down to his fingertips.

Adding to his growing misery and resentment, he frequently found himself asking his partner to help him pull sweaters and T-shirts on over his head, because he could only lift his left arm about three quarters of the way up, before being painfully reminded that nerves and muscles once connected the way nature intended, no longer were.

As fate would have it, the days when Barn was hurting the most physically always coincided with the days Arnie was hurting the most psychologically, and one wrong word from either partner would lead to a screaming match that only ended when the participants were too hoarse to continue.

Both of them had been warned about Post-Traumatic Stress Syndrome, but like a lot of young people, they felt invincible. The almost endless streak of bad luck they had been riding on had not seemed able to break either of their spirits—at least not completely—so they sucked it up, and kept going.

They had continued with the 'everything is great' charade until last New Year's Eve, when the steamroller that their long pent-up emotions had become, unexpectedly careened out of control.

Returning from a holiday visit to the Fentnors' Connecticut home only the previous day, Arnie had woken up around nine o'clock that morning, and stared at the ceiling for at least an hour. It seemed to have become a wide-screen projection TV for all of the horrendous events he had lived through.

On its flat, colorless surface he could see the shooting, his brother's funeral, his own confrontation with his brother's killer, and the host of other events that had conspired to create the worst spring of his life.

With Barn already at the studio, Arnie was alone with the horror show of his memories and with the terrifyingly cold, empty feeling that everything in his entire life had unraveled, and he would never get it back in order again.

The next day a new year would begin. Suddenly overwhelmed by the sickening thrill ride his emotions were taking him on, Arnie was sure that he did not want to be in it.

Barn would be home toward the middle of the afternoon; Arnie did not even care that his diminutive life partner would probably have a heart attack when he discovered his lifeless body.

Dragging himself to the bathroom, he groped around in the medicine cabinet for the necessary item, filled the tub with hot water, and climbed in.

The razor had not hurt as it slit his wrists.

> <

All four members of the band Barn was working with that morning, Oxidized Asylum, were gifted with the melodious voice of a warthog—but their name was worse.

He had no idea what image they were trying to conjure up with a moniker like that, but it made him think of a rusty tool shed.

Adding fuel to his already blazingly bad mood—his shoulder had been aching relentlessly since he woke up—he flipped the talk button on the control room mike into the 'ON' position, but felt no more than a dull pressure on his fingertips.

The almost total lack of sensation infuriated him, and, in a flustered 'straw that broke the camel's back' voice, he snapped, "Take a break."

Seated beside him at the consol, the producer, Bob Knox, looked toward him. Bob had been able to see for several months that his young engineer was slowly going down in flames, but every time he mentioned something, the younger man would deny there was a problem. Bob knew he had to crack eventually, and was not surprised by what happened next.

Grabbing the nearest object at hand, a headset, Barn viciously hurled it toward the wall, where it produced an oddly satisfying 'thump', before bouncing back out to the middle of the room.

Barn kicked it out of his way as he stomped toward the door. Yanking it open, he fired back over his shoulder, "You handle this, Bob. I'm outta here."

Hitting the street a few minutes later, Barn was shocked to see almost no mid-morning traffic. "Yippee," he thought irreverently. "A holiday miracle."

> <

"Hey, Arnie, I'm home."

With only silence echoing back in his ears, Barn suddenly felt afraid. It was time to stop pretending they were doing great, and admit that they were in dire need of help. What if it was already too late?

"Babe…where are you?" he called, running through the first floor of their condo, checking each room for his beloved partner—he found no trace of him.

Dashing wildly toward the stairs to the second floor, he took them two at a time, and burst into their bedroom. A cursory glance told him Arnie was not in the room.

The bathroom door was open, and steam wafted out onto the cooler air currents in the bedroom.

Despite the dread that tried to hold him back, an 80-proof shot of adrenalin raced through his system, and Barn rocketed toward the door.

It was a legitimate holiday miracle after all. Arnie was still breathing.

Dialing 911 with fingers that felt as though they belonged to ten different hands, Barn reached an operator, and reported that he had just found his partner in a bathtub full of hot water and warm blood, both of which were currently running down the drain.

Paramedics were at the scene in minutes, and Arnie was raced to the hospital, where he availed himself of the blood supply.

Another holiday miracle—a lot more people give blood during the holidays than during the rest of the year.

Chapter 3

Pulling his car into the poorly lit parking lot at the Honeybees 'n Raspberries Inn, Barn commented, "Leave the suitcases until after we check in, right?"

Arnie nodded, and answered, "Right."

The two young men climbed out of the car, stretching to get the kinks out of their backs and legs. It was a long drive up, but, between talking and thinking, the time had gone by quickly; without meaning to, they had made the entire trip without benefit of a single rest stop.

Walking slowly across the large, grassy parking area toward the inn's double doors, his partner just a step behind him, Barn turned to ask, "Hey, did I tell you I ran into Detective Mallory the other day?"

Arnie raised a golden brow, and said, "No…yesterday, ya' mean? Where?"

"Yeah…yesterday," Barn answered. "He was behind me in the check-out lane at Greenwood's."

Greenwood's Grocery was located in one of Lawton's middle-class neighborhoods and was only about a block away from the modest residence Barn's parents called home.

The little 'Mom and Pop' operation still employed Barn's parents at night, although on fewer evenings than it once had. During Barn's childhood, his parents worked there every night after putting in a full day at the post office.

"Whose lane…your mother's or your father's?" Arnie asked.

"Ma's lane—she was the only one working last night. Freddie and Dad went to a concert together." Dark eyes glistening with humor, he said, "Guess who they saw."

"No idea."

The young recording engineer smiled at his partner, and then asked, "Remember Boyd & Barton…or was it Barton & Boyd?" Looking only slightly puzzled, he laughed freely at his own inability to remember the names of the two young country singers who had given him fits last year.

"Is your brother a fan, or your father…or both?"

"Neither, I hope," Barn chuckled. "The two clowns, not Dad and Freddie, the other two, were opening for someone else. I forget who…whom…someone Dad likes."

The tall blond man grinned broadly and suggested, "Floyd Ledbedder and his all Harmonica Band?"

Barn laughed at the fictitious name, and then said, "Yeah, or someone equally bad, but getting back to seeing Mallory…"

"Sorry, I didn't mean to get us off track," Arnie interrupted.

Grinning, Barn answered, "It's OK, babe…all I was really gonna say was that I saw him, and he asked how everyone was doing."

With a quick sideways glance at his partner, the dark-haired man added, "I told him your folks moved to Pennsylvania…no memories there."

Detective Kyle Mallory would know all about the Kotkins' memories. He had answered the call about the shooting at the hospital the night of Joseph Kotkin's heart attack, and his car had been the first one on the scene of Jerry's automobile crash.

Late one night, when Arnie and Barn realized that the two incidents were part of the same picture, and not the unrelated tragedies they appeared to be, it was Kyle Mallory they had called with the information; the detective knew all about the Kotkin family's troubles.

Arnie kicked at a bit of gravel in the predominantly grass parking lot. "He heard about me back in January, I imagine." He did not like to think that the detective who had been impressed by his cleverness also knew he had attempted suicide.

"Probably" Barn began nonchalantly, "but we didn't talk about it…I mean, I certainly didn't say, 'Hey, know what? Arnie tried to check out early'…but when I dialed 911 that morning, half the city heard about you—the emergency services anyway."

Intuitively, he added, "But don't worry about it…you're not the only person who ever reached their breaking point a lot sooner than they ever thought they would."

"Funny, in a way…right after you got shot, I told you we had to talk everything out, but I'm the one who was bottling most of it up," Arnie mused aloud.

Hands in his jeans pockets, Barn shrugged. "I did my share of bottling" he admitted, "but you had a lot more to deal with than I did. I'm the one who got shot, but the rest of that stuff happened to you."

They reached the badly peeling doors, and headed inside.

><

Standing in the small foyer when the doors swung open, George Parker, a lousy innkeeper and worse human being, eyed the two young men suspiciously. They were not touching each other, but there was an air of intimate familiarity between them. "We're full," he growled.

George Parker hated the general public, and he made no bones about it. Until last summer when his wife, Bessie, died, he had not needed to bother with the inn. This place was the friendly, gentle Bessie's pride and joy not his; he cared so little that he left the renovations she had begun unfinished after her death.

Furthering his claim to the 'Scum of the Year' title, he had put the place his wife loved so dearly on the market the day before her funeral. There were no takers for some months, but it looked as though there was one now.

He had not met with a representative yet, but The Yantzing Development Company had begun to put out feelers, and he had shown that he was eager to work with them.

In one of their representative's many phone calls to him, he was told that they wanted to put in a mall; it was all hush-hush right now.

George Parker did not care if Yantzing wanted the land for a crematorium—he just wanted to be rid of it.

The cantankerous old innkeeper liked his regular part-time job over at Myles Buck's service station up the road a lot better than he liked being an innkeeper. He was a mechanic by trade and, despite his 61 years, he was an incredibly strong man.

Parker had already made plans to move into the tiny apartment above Myles' garage after he sold out. The single room and small bath would serve his needs.

"We have a reservation," Arnie told the grouch in the foyer. "The name is Kotkin, Arnold Kotkin. I booked it at least a month ago."

"More like two, Arnie," Barn said.

Parker crossed to the tiny podium that held the reservations book, a telephone and a few pencils. He studied the book for a minute; the name was there.

He looked up at the two young men again. The blond was of age, he was sure of that. Himself 6' tall, Parker estimated that Kotkin probably had six inches on him, but several pounds less. The innkeeper thought he looked like a starved weasel; he thought the other guy looked about ready for 6th grade.

"Let's see some ID," he snorted.

Barn produced his driver's license without a word.

Parker studied it intently—same too-long dark hair, dark eyes, and childlike features. The date of birth was November 9, 1978—almost 26 years earlier.

He handed the ID back to the young man.

"All right, I've got it" he admitted, the dull tone of his voice making it clear that he was disappointed to find 'Kotkin/2' written on the book. "Confirm your phone number for me," he growled.

Arnie rattled off the number for his cell phone, and then said, "Do you take American Express?"

"A'ya, I take that one; it pays slower than hell, but I take it," Parker grumbled, snatching the plastic card away from its owner. "Room's $72 a night. Get out of the room by 11:30, and don't come back until seven at night."

Barn began, "What time's break…"

"Nine o'clock," Parker cut him off sharply. "I only serve once."

Chapter 4

Three walls of the fair-sized bedroom were covered with whitewashed, ash paneling. The fourth wall was off-white plaster, covered with distressed latticework; the visual effect it provided was interesting, albeit dust-catching.

The room's only window, hung with an indigo-tinted sheer panel curtain that closely matched the shade of the rug, looked out across a wide expanse of lawn toward a small tavern on the opposite side of the green.

Located just off the bedroom, in what had once been a walk-in closet, an adequate bathroom showed off modern fixtures and jaunty, nautical-themed wallpaper, but its black-and-white tiled floor was cracked in several places.

Looking around the room, Arnie observed, "Um, nice room…or it should be."

Remembering the overgrown parking area and the peeling front doors, he added, "It looks like someone cared a lot about this whole place once, but not anymore."

Continuing to study his new surroundings, the young, blond man said, "I get the feeling someone started some pretty extensive renovations, but never finished."

Putting his suitcase down on the room's obviously ancient brass bed, he quipped, "I didn't know they made king-sized beds 200 years ago." Unzipping his jacket, and tossing it on the bed over the suitcase, he speculated, "I'll bet all the furniture was slated for replacement pretty soon…these aren't antiques, they're just crap."

Unable to lift his own suitcase high enough to put it on the bed, courtesy of the old gunshot wound, Barn set it down on the floor before giving the other furniture in their temporary living quarters a closer look.

"I agree with you there, babe," he said. "This stuff's decrepit, but not valuable." Eyeing a particularly ugly chest of drawers in one corner of the room, and unbuttoning his cardigan sweater at the same time, Barn commented, "I'm pretty sure no one's used this color stain in a long time. Armoires shouldn't be orange."

Arnie looked toward the dresser his partner was referring to, and wrinkled his nose; clearly the old ginger tint, once so popular, did not meet with his approval either. He sat down in a straight-backed chair near the door. It creaked threateningly, and he shot back to his feet. "Great" he muttered, "I hope the bed's not this bad."

Not yet worrying about the condition of the mattress, Barn was still taking in the other sights in the room. "The TV doesn't look promising," he observed.

He turned to glance toward the head of the massive, old bed. A chipped and scarred mahogany table standing guard beside it held an equally ancient chimney lamp—amazingly enough, it also held a digital clock—but nothing else.

"Not even a remote," Barn said dejectedly.

Like all men born since the invention of the sacred instrument of channel control, Barn, an otherwise intelligent man, could not comprehend so much as the weather report, unless he was holding the remote control; with Arnie suffering from the same malady, the news hour could get ugly.

"Shit…that's a bummer," Arnie commented. His attention still drawn to the crappy furniture in a room that, clearly, had seen a lot of restoration work, he ruminated aloud, "I wonder why he never finished renovating."

With his own mind still on the unfortunate situation with the remote control, Barn made the half-hearted comment, "Maybe this is the look he was going for."

Suddenly remembering Arnie's remark vis-à-vis the bed not being as bad as the room's lone chair, Barn decided to check the mattress for comfort.

Rather than take a running start from the other side of the room, he used his suitcase as a stepstool to climb aboard the bed.

In seconds, he was crawling along a mattress lumpy enough to pass for an enormous sack of potatoes. "I'll be sleeping on top of you tonight, babe," he commented drolly.

Noticing the 'come again' look his partner immediately directed his way he amended, "I didn't mean that. I meant you're probably more comfortable to sleep on than some people…mattresses…I mean mattresses."

"Keep talking, Barn. The more you say, the worse it sounds," Arnie grinned. "You started with just one foot in your mouth; try for both of 'em…see if you can swallow yourself."

Standing beside the bed when he began to speak, Arnie ended up sitting on the edge of the mattress; the comment he tried to deliver seriously, broke him up when he got a surprisingly vivid mental picture of his tiny partner doing exactly that—and disappearing forever with only the slightest popping sound.

"I used to be really good with words," his small dark-haired companion complained, not understanding that his partner was laughing at himself. "I don't know why I can't string three words together lately without sounding stupid."

Settling back on the bed, he continued to snicker at both his own comment and what he thought was Arnie's reaction to it.

Standing an even 5' tall, and weighing a whopping 108 pounds, Barn had room to spare in a twin-sized bed, but in his new quarters, probably the first king-sized bed ever made, he looked like a pine needle.

He stretched out and rolled around a bit, seeking maximum comfort, or any comfort at all, on Methuselah's former mattress.

Watching his impish partner fondly, Arnie commented, "You look lost on a bed this big, Barney. Doesn't he have a spare pea pod or something that you could sleep in?" He leaned over to give Barn's longish, dark hair a gentle tussle.

Barn reached one hand up to grasp Arnie's wrist, pulled it toward his lips and gently kissed the 10-month-old scars. The tender moment was broken by his unexpected announcement. "I gotta hit the can."

Arnie burst out laughing. "Anyone else lucky enough to be alone in a bedroom with me would be thinking of something other than their bladder," he finally said.

Still stretched out on his back, Barn giggled, "You quit therapy too soon, babe. Go back to see Dr. Rupert for a refresher course; I think you're delusional."

No offense was intended, or taken. It would have been impossible for Arnie to be offended by his partner's joke; after all, he was following the doctor's orders.

One of the most valuable lessons Anne Wilhelm Rupert, Ph.D. had taught them was so simple it almost sounded silly. 'How scary can anything be…how hard can it be to face…when it's laughable'?

It had taken many months, because laughter was not high up on their list of priorities after the day Arnie had done a mercifully poor job of slashing his wrists, but over time, both had seen the intrinsic wisdom of Dr. Rupert's words.

The easy, teasing banter they had enjoyed in the early days of their relationship had returned, and they were both better for it.

"I'm not…" Arnie began as an unexpected yawn interrupted his thought. He concluded a second later, "delusional…I think I'm more in the mood for a nap."

Barn quickly moved, pointing to the spot he had just vacated. "Don't take my spot. It's the only comfortable place on the entire bed…and watch out that you don't kick your suitcase. I didn't have that problem, because my legs aren't long enough to reach it."

He scrambled off the bed, and scuttled toward the bathroom.

Watching his partner disappear into the nautically themed lavatory, Arnie called out, "Don't worry about it, I'd like for more than my kneecap to be comfortable."

By the time Barn returned from the bathroom, Arnie had, nevertheless, captured the prime location.

Climbing back onto the bed, looking like a mop-haired mouse scaling a mountain of cheddar, Barn directed, "Find your own spot, Arnie…that's mine."

Reasoning that it was better to move than listen to Barn complain until Halloween, Arnie moved over to the bed's left side. Stretching his lanky form out, he knew he had made a mistake—the bed's only comfortable spot was the one he had just given up without a fight.

Barn, whose comfortable spot was dead center on the mattress, rolled over to cuddle against his friend. "Do you really want to take a nap, Arnie?" he asked. "What happened to all that crap about how lucky I am to be alone in a bedroom with you?" He stretched his arms up around the other man's neck, pressing his lips against the warm, silky skin below his left ear.

"That's not exactly what I said," Arnie corrected, with a feigned air of superiority, trying at the same time to ignore the warm, moist tongue that was busily exploring his earlobe. "I said anyone lucky enough to be alone in a bedroom with me..."

The bed's tiny occupant cut the taller one off in mid-sentence. "What other lucky people are there, Arnie? I've been sleeping with you for over a year now, and no one's ever tapped me on the shoulder in the middle of the night asking to cut in."

The bed shook with Arnie's laughter. "If you think I'm gonna even touch you after a crack like that, take another think."

Face still pressed to the side of his partner's neck, Barn began unbuttoning Arnie's shirt. "Come on," he whispered, his warm breath causing the other man to shiver. "I didn't move over here because I was cold."

Chapter 5

The small, brass bell hanging over the door of the White Star Tavern jingled at precisely 9:30 Sunday night.

Gretchen Grissom, the tall, silver-haired proprietor of the tavern, looked up from last week's edition of 'The Grove Gazette'. The local paper came out on Saturday afternoons, and carried the news of the week gone by—not that there was ever much news to carry. Maple Grove Junction was a dull place, except in the fall, when the leaf peepers showed up.

The old barkeeper delighted in seeing a new throng of leaf peepers every year, when the surrounding hills exchanged summer's blanket of unbroken green for autumn's glorious dream coat of red, yellow and orange. Thanks to their fresh eyes, Gretchen saw her surroundings anew each fall, and reveled in them.

Every year, she wished one of the leaf peepers would make her see Whit Grissom's ugly mug and fading red hair with new eyes—but, so far, no luck. Her husband was just as ugly now, as he had been when she had married him 45 years ago. Truth to tell, he was worse—at least in those days the skin under his chin had fit snuggly. Today, it was three sizes too big.

The most obvious advantage to running a tavern during what Gretchen called, "leaf peeper season" was that they all seemed to be an incredibly thirsty bunch. Whoever they were, and wherever they came from, they all seemed to enjoy a cold Bud at the end of the day, and she served it with a smile and a clink of silver in the cash drawer.

Now 65, and still as feisty and gregarious as she had been at 20, Gretchen enjoyed the leaf peepers for more than their patronage. A woman who could engage a walnut in conversation, she loved to get the leaf peepers talking about their homes, families and occupations; their stories made for a more enjoyable tête-à-tête than news about Whit Grissom's damned prostate.

No matter what the season, Gretchen could always rely on seeing the familiar faces of her steadiest customers every day—even if their company did get old fast.

Joe Burns and Dick Miller, first cousins and best friends, were both retired forestry workers. They came in before noon most days, and stayed until closing time talking, drinking and playing poker with Whit Grissom.

The cousins, as most people in the Grove called Joe and Dick, had moved from Maine to Vermont about a dozen years ago, after leaving the Forestry Service.

Both men often made the typical old timers' joke about taking up space in their golden years; just as often, Gretchen told them the only space they ever took up was in her tavern.

The old men never tired of their one-liner, but after a full day of it, Gretchen was ready to jump off the roof.

Myles Buck, who ran the Grove's only service station, came in as soon as his 'part-time kid', George Parker, got to the station around noon; he also stayed until closing.

Myles, whose oddly shaped face had always reminded Gretchen of a turnip, was another life-long resident of Vermont. At the age of 25, he had taken over the reins of the small service station up on Route 5. It had been in his family for at least 80 years when he took over; it had racked up 45 more years since then, and Myles was still at the helm.

Myles Buck put in a half day at the station, and a full night at the tavern.

In the last quarter century, not more than two consecutive nights had passed without Myles reminding Gretchen that his father used to give her salted peanuts from a small canister he kept in the station's grimy office; it was his way of telling her that he was entitled to more than his fair share of free nuts and pretzels from the bar.

Tonight, the four toothless geezers were seated at their usual table near the fireplace. Supposedly they were playing poker, but the woman behind the bar suspected none of them even knew the rules. They spent more time gossiping like old women than they did passing out cards; they even talked more than they drank, which was saying something—especially for Whit and Myles.

Her two newest visitors were not locals, but Gretchen was sure they were not ordinary leaf peepers either. Even at night, leaf peepers often came in wearing binoculars and cameras around their necks like strange tribal necklaces; the two young men who passed through the big oak door had nothing but collars around their necks.

The taller of the two men wore dark corduroy pants, a leather jacket with his shirt collar poking out at the top, and black leather boots; the second man was clad in faded jeans, a concert type T-shirt with a bulky, green cardigan sweater over it, and sneakers.

While there was nothing overtly feminine about either of them, Gretchen—like George Parker before her—had an immediate sense of the contented intimacy between them; her reaction was a far cry from what the belligerent innkeeper's had been.

'God bless the liberals in Vermont' she thought. Despite the age bracket she fell into, Gretchen Grissom was a free spirit. As she saw it, if folks wanted to be legally united, they should be able to—assuming neither of the parties to a new union were still the parties to an old one. 'If they're not a couple up here to get hitched' she thought, 'I'll run to the back table, and kiss Whit Grissom…ugly old bastard.'

"What'll it be, boys?" she asked the two young men, as they seated themselves at the bar.

The skinny blond answered, "Whatever's on tap…and can I get a sandwich? I don't care what kind."

He was a pleasant looking man, Gretchen thought, and he had beautiful eyes—he just needed some meat on his bones. She watched as he reached for the small basket of cocktail peanuts at the end of the bar, and then nibbled a few.

"Bud's on tap, and I can fix ya' a cheese sandwich. How's that?" the woman asked. "The four old fools at the back table cleaned me out of ham and roast beef. I'll be getting a delivery tomorrow, but right now, it's cheese or nothing." She chuckled, adding, "How they're chewing that meat's a mystery to me. They don't have six teeth between 'em."

Arnie liked the old woman; she reminded him of his aunt. "Sounds fine," he said. "Thanks."

Gretchen turned her lively blue eyes on the second man. If he was up here to get hitched, he was old enough to drink, she figured—but she would have to ask for his ID

41

in a minute anyway; he barely looked 12 years old. "How about you?" she asked him.

"Heineken…and a cheese sandwich sounds good to me too," he answered. "I'm starving."

"None of those fancy names, here…it's Bud, take it or leave it; show me some ID before you take it."

The dark-haired young man on the other side of the bar produced his driver's license for the second time since arriving in Maple Grove Junction, and passed it across the bar.

Gretchen studied it for a minute before returning it to its rightful owner.

"Almost 26?" she queried, passing the license back. "Little, ain't ya'?" she said. Never one to be politically correct, for she reasoned that if any two words could be defined as antonyms, 'political' and 'correct' had to be the ones, she always spoke her mind.

"Not that little," Barn answered frankly, meeting her eyes with devilment in his own. Like his partner, he had taken an immediate liking to the woman behind the bar.

No one who knew her could deny that Gretchen Grissom had a sense of humor, with the possible exception of George Parker, who hated her as much as she hated him. Immediately grasping the intended meaning of the double entendre, she said with a lusty laugh, "If you think you're big enough, good for you."

Pulling off the two beers, and putting them on the bar, she said, "I'll be right back with your sandwiches…kitchen's out back." She turned briskly, and disappeared into a smaller room behind the bar.

Arnie chuckled. "Until she answered, I almost couldn't believe I'd heard you say that," he said. Ready to slide the small basket closer to his friend, he casually asked, "Peanut?"

"Don't call me that," Barn answered, his eyes still on the door through which their hostess had departed.

His companion burst out laughing. "I was offering you these," Arnie finally said, lightly tapping the basket. "When have I ever called you 'Peanut'?"

Barn's ability to laugh at himself had always been a trait Arnie admired, and he was laughing now.

Still grinning broadly a few seconds later, he admitted, "I wasn't paying attention to what you were doing."

"Well, pay attention to me. The sandwiches won't get out here any faster with you staring at the door, drooling like a Saint Bernard."

The hungry young man said, "I'm not drooling." With a resigned shake of his dark head, he added, "I've just stuck myself with a horrible nickname…like that kid we went to school with…I can't even remember his actual name…"

Even as his voice trailed away, Barn's dark eyes shone with amusement at another page from their joint book of boyhood memories.

"Chunky Goldman?" Arnie suggested, popping another nut into his mouth.

"Yeah, that's him," Barn agreed with a laugh. "His mother never named him 'Chunky'…you did that. What was his real name? I can't think of it."

Munching on a few more peanuts, Arnie pondered the question, finally coming up with the name. "Irving," he announced. "It was Irving Goldman…and up until then, his friends all called him Goldie…which was worse than Chunky, if you ask me."

Eyes twinkling, Barn said, "It wasn't as creative, that's for sure." He ate some nuts, and then continued, "I remember him bugging me at recess that day…the day you renamed him. He kept calling me half-pint and a couple other things…not very original stuff, as I recall, but he was torturing me just the same, and his flunkies thought it was hysterical."

"I remember that day too," Arnie said, thinking back over Barn's illustrious career as a miniature schoolyard thug, and himself as the loyal sidekick and straight man; it was odd that in later years Arnie should have become the one who had the hardest time keeping a straight face.

"I think we got the longest detention ever given out in the history of PS 148..." he began.

"Yeah" Barn interrupted, "because I punched him so hard in the stomach that he threw up, and you called him Chunky." He still sounded oddly proud of the accomplishment that had earned them three solid weeks of detention.

It was also the achievement that won his backend a personal introduction to his father's belt. The unhappy get-together had been threatened many times in the past, because Barn was no stranger to hitting back, but it was not until the petite scrapper had actually thrown the first punch in a schoolyard altercation that leather met denim.

As the belt had finally left its happy home around his father's waist, the 11-year-old mischief-maker had frantically pled his case—it was wrong to hit him as punishment for hitting someone else.

Larry Moss had taken a different view. He believed that loving parents did not threaten a punishment, and then continually fail to follow through with it; children had to learn that for every action, good or bad, there was a reaction.

His belt had swung once through the air, and made a nice 'snappy' sound on the seat of his young son's jeans; Barn had been far more embarrassed than hurt.

His partner's voice mockingly called him back to the present, "Funny how nicknames stick, isn't it...Peanut?"

'Peanut' Moss ignored the remark, and said, "The way she talks kind of reminds me of Mrs. Fentnor...the wisecracks, ya' know? Your aunt's a lot prettier, though."

Even though Barn had known Helene Fentnor since he was a 7-year-old boy and loved her almost like he loved his own mother, he still addressed his partner's biological mother as 'Mrs. Fentnor', and frequently still referred to her as Arnie's aunt.

"I agree," Arnie replied, his hazel eyes surveying the interior of the small tavern.

Dimly lit, more to save on the light bill than to create ambiance, the White Star's main room was nonetheless inviting.

The fire roaring in the stone fireplace at the back of the room filled the place with cedar-scented warmth, and a good supply of firewood was neatly stacked in the corner.

The walls were hung with old, hand-painted road signs and large, roughly framed photographs of the Vermont landscape. A moose head, capped with a ridiculous red stocking cap, surveyed the room from above the mantel.

Licking salt from his fingertips, Arnie said, "It's a comfortable place, but can you imagine my mother sitting here? God, what would people say?"

"I can't get a mental picture of Mrs. K here, no," Barn admitted with a smile.

It took no effort at all to picture the wealthy but down-to-earth Fentnors sitting in this room; Helene would be sitting here at the bar talking amiably, while Jack played poker with the 'boys' near the fireplace.

"Mrs. Fentnor would probably be the one who put that stupid hat on the moose," Barn laughed.

Arnie grinned at the idea, and then looked toward the old poker players again; hunched silently over their cards, they looked frozen in time. He noted, "Either they've all died back there, or they forgot whose turn it is."

Chuckling, he clarified, "Hold on, hold on...I think I see one of 'em moving his lips. He must be telling the others a story."

Barn looked back toward the men, and then grinned at his partner, "It's not a very exciting one...they all look pretty bored."

"They must've heard it before," Arnie grinned.

"And they'd remember?" his tiny counterpart laughed merrily. With his next breath, he admitted, "I should watch myself; that'll be us in 50 years."

"God, take my hair if you want it, but leave me my teeth," Arnie quipped, and both men laughed.

Changing the subject, the young blond man queried, "Think we should ask the bartender how to get to the town hall, or wait to ask Mr. Personality back at the inn?"

Barn's answer came before his heart beat once.

"She's the one to ask," he said, remembering the dour face of the man who had checked them in a few hours earlier. "He wasn't all that friendly, was he?"

It was a gross understatement.

"Not really," Arnie agreed. Pursing his lips in annoyance, he said, "I guess not all Vermonters approve of same-sex marriages. He was definitely not happy when he found my name on that book...he'd probably written 'Mr. and Mrs. Kotkin'. He's pissed about us being there; I could see it in his eyes."

He snickered suddenly, saying, "It must have killed him to ask for my phone number...he was probably afraid I'd take it as a proposition." He shrugged his shoulders at his own foolish suggestion.

Quizzically, Barn said, "Why'd he need the number anyway? I showed ID, and you gave him a perfectly good credit card."

Arnie raised his brows, and let out a slow breath. "I don't really know, I suppose I should have asked, but his attitude threw me," he admitted. "It's probably just a security thing, or in case we forget something in the room."

Barn nodded; it was a reasonable assumption.

Dark eyes continuing to scan the small room, Barn soon found himself watching the four old men at the table near the fireplace again as they talked, drank and played no poker.

After a minute, he quizzed, "I wonder if this is a local hot spot?"

"A'ya," Gretchen said, returning to the bar, the paper plates in her hands making Barn feel even more at home. His mother always served on Dixie.

"Up here, if you're open past nine o'clock, folks figure you're hot. This time of year" she joked, "we're a regular tourist trap, 'cept on Sunday nights. It's always quiet then…danged if I know why. There's still the same number of motels just off the interstate."

Plopping the plates unceremoniously before her smiling patrons, she cautioned, "Watch the cheese, I just nuked 'em. Got a microwave a couple days ago—I still ain't used to the danged thing."

She glanced toward the back of the room. "I figure if Whit Grissom gets too much more ornery than he already is, I'll nuke him some night…old bastard."

The young men glanced back toward the non-poker game again.

"Which one is Whit Grissom?" Barn asked, thinking none of them looked particularly charming.

"The ugly old bastard in the red shirt…looks about as smart as cow manure," she said, indicating the table's lone speaker.

Barn agreed with her assessment, but said reasonably, "As long as he can pay his tab, I guess you really don't have to like him."

"Hell" Gretchen said, "I'm married to the ugly old fool, but I guess there's no point whining about it; no one twisted my arm." The slight twitching at the corners of her mouth negated the sentiment of her words.

Gretchen Grissom may have called her husband an ugly old bastard—God, the man was repulsive—and insinuated he was no smarter than shit, but she was glad he was here.

A lot of women her age were widows already, and last year, when he had suffered the heart attack that led to his triple bypass surgery, she had been afraid she would be joining that unfortunate group; there was no logical reason for it, but she loved the old bastard.

The spry old tavern proprietor made sure her husband walked every day, ate a well-balanced diet and got plenty of rest. She babied him, and he ate it up with a spoon.

Long since released to resume his normal course of physical activity, which had never been much in the first place—unless watching Gretchen support him constituted activity—he still let her do everything from mowing the lawn and chopping firewood, to stacking provisions in the storeroom and working at the bar.

An amazingly strong woman, whose fierce determination counted for as much as her physical strength, Gretchen Grissom could do more bull work than some people half her age; when she did need a hand with something, she called on Russ Johnson, the resident state trooper, who was a damned good carpenter and a jack-of-all-trades.

"I inherited this place from my folks," the old woman said. "I never put any of it in Whit's name, though. I was afraid the drunken old bastard would lose it at cards; he can't play worth crap...stupid bastard."

Shaking her head as though disgusted with her husband's behavior, but smiling affectionately at the same time, she confided, "I never saw a man as bad at cards as he is. Stupid

51

bastard's bad at everything he puts his hand to, come to think of it...not that he puts his hand to much. Anyway, I've been here all my life. Whit Grissom and I live above the tavern now. It's just a little place, but it's where I grew up...went to school just down the road a piece."

She cocked her head toward the back of the room again, and said, "I snagged the old bastard right here at this bar. Drunken fool used to come in here every night...he swept me off my feet. God, I must have been half plowed myself to ever think he was good-looking, but I did."

With a grin, she admitted, "He talked like no one I'd ever heard before. We don't generally use the King's English up here...or maybe it's the Queen's now...but he almost doesn't use English at all...not that you'd recognize anyway."

More seriously, she added, "Just after we got hitched, both my folks got sick—Ma had kidney troubles and Pa had cancer."

Smiling proudly at her husband's responsible and loving behavior, the old woman said, "Whit nursed 'em like they were his own people, and not just his in-laws. He's good that way...he was pretty broken up when they died."

She heaved a heavy sigh, and then acknowledged, "Old bastard cheated on me one time...nearly 25 years ago now..."

"Oh?" the audience of two said, surprised by the totally unexpected, and extremely personal, revelation.

Gretchen laughed, turning the momentary soul baring into a joke. "We get the occasional desperate woman up in these parts every quarter-century or so, but other than that, he's not a bad old coot." She smirked, and said, "Just uglier than a barrel of boiled assholes."

"He is pretty ugly" Barn agreed, not really knowing what else to say. He had heard some colorful descriptions, but that topped pretty much everything.

Gretchen nodded, suddenly wiping eyes that surprised her by growing glassy with unexpected tears. "The tavern and him are the only things I can call my own in this life," she acknowledged. "We never had any kids, but they probably would've turned out ugly like him anyway, so I guess it's just as well."

The joke at her husband's expense brought a smile back to her face, and she extended a hand to her new patrons, saying, "I'm Gretchen Grissom. I can't believe I didn't say my own name before now; living with Whit Grissom's making my brain go soft."

Arnie introduced himself, and then, jerking his thumb in Barn's direction, added, "Barney Moss, my partner."

"Thanks for the enthusiastic introduction," Barn said. He took no offense, though; Arnie was more inclined to be at a loss for words sometimes than he was.

The post-grad student laughed, suddenly self-conscious. "You're welcome."

The woman behind the bar easily swept Arnie's momentary awkwardness aside with a few simple words.

"Nice to know ya', boys," she said.

Eyes flashing in the direction of the smaller man, she added, "I already knew Barney's name...I just checked his ID."

She smiled again, and asked pointblank "Come up to get hitched, did ya'?"

Just as directly, Barn responded, "Yeah...at two o'clock on Wednesday. We have to get the license on Monday..."

"Need blood tests?" Gretchen interrupted.

Barn laughed. "We got 'em done at home, and brought a copy of the results with us to be on the safe side, but we don't honestly know. We tried checking online 'cuz we couldn't get through on the phone..."

"Town hall's hours are irregular," Gretchen commented. "Not busy enough around here to merit being open every day. You probably just hit 'em on days when they were closed...they don't have that fancy voice mail stuff."

With a brief nod of acknowledgement for the statement, Barn continued, "Must be that. Anyway, we did find out that some places require blood tests and some don't. For some reason, it stands out in my mind that Ontario doesn't have a blood test requirement…"

Arnie cut in, "But we couldn't connect to the server with the Vermont information, though."

Reclaiming his story, Barn stated, "We kept getting a message saying that we weren't authorized to view that page. Go figure."

"Just as well to get 'em then," Gretchen said. "Now, do you know how to get to the town hall?"

Barn grinned, "That was gonna be my next question."

The old woman answered, "Go out the door here, hitch a left, go down the road a piece, and you'll run right into it…big brick place it is. It's got white double doors, and a white gazebo out front. You'll find it."

Having a bit more information to impart, Gretchen pulled a stool over, and sat down across the bar from the two young men; she always kept a stool there, because the tavern's only phone was beneath the bar, and she was the only one who answered it.

"Now" she began, "when you get there on Monday, you'll go into the Town Clerk's office on the first floor—they'll help ya' out with the license. When you go back on Wednesday, you'll go up to the second floor…Probate Court's up there. Have you got witnesses? If you don't, me and the old bastard can do it."

"Thanks, we're all set on witnesses…Arnie's aunt and uncle will be up sometime Tuesday" Barn said, before asking, "How far is 'a piece'?"

Gretchen smiled at the dark-haired man. "Ain't ever clocked it," she said, her grammar sounding like her husband's. "In this case, I guess I'd say it's too big a piece for you to walk without blistering your feet, but plenty short enough to make it in the car without blistering your backside."

"How long does it take to get there?" Arnie asked.

"Give yourselves 20 minutes or so to get there from here, I guess…it'll allow you a little time in case you hit some leaf peeper traffic."

After offering that suggestion, she added, "The Grove's a big town as they go 'round these parts…not that there's ever been anything much here," she mused aloud to the young men.

"It's very pretty," Barn observed, while Arnie nodded his agreement.

Her voice taking on an impassioned edge, Gretchen said, "It's always been nice and peaceful…the locals like it this way, and the tourists do too. Lately, some jackass has taken the notion to start building here." She shook her silvery head with disgust, adding, "There's plenty of empty space for 'em to use—no need to go putting people outta their places."

"Progress sucks," Arnie said.

Gretchen nodded, and gave the young man a wink. "Smart boy," she said.

Continuing with her instructions about the procedure for Wednesday, she expounded, "Judge Pratty'll do the ceremony. He's been probate judge ever since Billy Hickman kicked off about this time last year. I never did like that man…Hickman, I mean. He had a heart attack right here in my tavern…"

"That's awful," Barn and Arnie interrupted in unison.

Gretchen continued, "For him, I suppose…not for anyone who knew him. He was a miserable son of a bitch; he hated everyone, and most of 'em hated him right back. Tell you the truth, I was surprised he lived long enough to die of natural causes."

"Sounds like someone I used to work with," Arnie commented, thinking of Howard Tucker, his former department head.

"Suppose we all know someone like that" Gretchen answered, before continuing, "Only good thing he ever did for me was drop dead here…it was great for business. Just around Halloween, it was. I remember folks were sitting around in here drinking beer and shootin' the shit, and all of a sudden, Hickman's dead on the floor...plop! Son of a bitch walked through the door, and fell down faster than Whit Grissom's...well, you get the idea."

Barn and Arnie exchanged surprised glances, but they laughed—poor Whit.

The barkeeper continued, "Next day, the old bastard put the word out that we'd heard Hickman's voice all night long. It was amazing how many people who hated the sound of Hickman's voice when he was alive, came back every night to hear it after he died."

After giving a hearty laugh, the old woman continued, "When they got drunk enough, I expect they did hear it, too." With a shake of her silver mane, she added, "For myself, I can't say I ever heard it...Whit Grissom probably did though...drunken old bastard."

Abruptly changing the topic, the old woman asked, "You boys staying 'cross the way at 'Honeybees'?"

"Yeah," Barn answered. "The guy who runs it doesn't really seem to show that much interest in it...aside from taking the money."

"Used to be a nicer place back when Bessie, George's wife, was alive," Gretchen explained.

Digging up more local gossip for the entertainment of her new patrons, Gretchen announced, "Bastard beat her, but

I could never get her to report it—not even to her niece's husband, Russ."

Then, describing a man who was already in his mid-40s, she added, "Nice boy, Russ is…he's our resident state trooper. I thought he might move on after his wife, Bessie's niece, passed away…lots of memories here, ya' know…but he's stayed on."

Lowering her voice to a whisper, and getting back to the subject of George Parker, she said, "I worry whenever I see women checking in alone over there." Nodding her head toward the tavern door as though it were a window, she explained, "He always puts 'em in the biggest room at the front."

Wondering how the location of the bedroom for women should be of interest to him, Barn casually remarked, "We're neighbors, then. Arnie and I are in the other front room."

"The room they're in is bigger" Gretchen informed him. "It's got twin beds. He always gives it to women traveling together…"

"Not to men?" Arnie asked, grinning. He knew his earlier supposition about Parker was right. He had to have thought Arnie would be showing up with a wife, or at least a girlfriend.

Gretchen understood the unasked question. "I don't know if Parker is homophobic or not…probably is. I think the situation's just never come up before…two men traveling together booking a room at his place."

"Is that room the only one with twin beds?" Barn asked, guessing that it must be.

"No, there's another," Gretchen said. She began to explain, "You know how the rooms are set up, two facing front, two facing the back…"

"Wide hallway in the middle" Barn smiled, adding his two cents worth to the description of the second story's floor plan.

"Exactly" Gretchen verified, nodding her head. "The room that's directly across from yours has twin beds; the other one has a king-sized bed."

"Sounds like you're pretty familiar with things," Arnie said. "Do you visit there often?"

Gretchen answered, "Hell, yes!"

After a quick glance around, she whispered, "I've still got the key Bessie gave me years ago, not that Parker knows about it. He never knew…no one did, 'cept for the old bastard." Cackling, the old woman said, "Didn't want him to think I was steppin' out myself."

After her comment got the desired laugh from her new patrons, she grew serious again, and reminisced, "Back when Bessie was alive, I'd go in after the lights were all out—sort of check things out for myself. I was always afraid I'd find her dead on the floor from him beating her, but the time I did find her, it was a heart attack that'd killed her." She looked toward the back of the tavern, but she was not seeing it.

After a few silent seconds slipped by, she informed her customers, "Right now, I know there's three women there. One's got a man with her, so she's safe enough."

Eyes darting around the room, ostensibly checking the dark corners for spies lurking there, she whispered, "I've seen 'em walking around the green a couple times...cranky looking sort he is." She snorted, "Makes ya' wanna shoot him...put him outta his misery."

Serious again, she explained, "The other two women are traveling together...they'd be in their 20s I guess."

Smiling suddenly, the old woman behind the counter said, "They've been in here every night since they got here... and that was on Thursday. They seem like nice enough girls...kinda funny, one of 'em is...she always wears a babushka..."

"A what?" Arnie asked.

Barn answered before the old woman could. "It's a scarf thing—a kerchief. Women wear 'em on their heads." He grinned, "Ma's got a couple...she forces 'em into service when her hair looks crappy."

"Oh," Arnie said. "So, what's funny about that?" he asked, looking back at the old woman behind the bar.

Gretchen shrugged, "I don't know, really…I just never saw a woman wearing one at night. You'll see 'em sometimes at the general store in the daytime, but not at night…not in the Grove anyway. Women 'round here wear regular hats at night—heavy ones this time of year."

Apparently, the Grove was a fashion giant.

"But" Gretchen continued, "what I wanted to say was they seem like they're just out looking for some harmless fun. Can you boys kinda keep an eye on 'em?"

Barn and Arnie traded glances again. This time, they were not wondering about "Little Whit's" rapid rate of decent— they were wondering if Mr. Personality would be better named Mr. Psychopath.

Arnie said, "If you think they're in danger, Mrs. Grissom, shouldn't you let your state trooper know about it?"

"I always tell him 'bout George Parker, and he says, 'Gretchen, you're where you are, and I'm where I am. You call me when you see him do something I can nail him for'. Folks who don't know, might think I'm nuts, but Russ knows. So, you boys just look sharp, and if you notice him giving either of those two girls the eye, or something like that, you just gimme a holler, OK? I can get Russ here in no time."

As she wrote her phone number on the back of a matchbook cover and handed it to them, Arnie and Barn nodded wordlessly.

Both men wondered what they might be letting themselves in for.

Chapter 6

The moon was nowhere in sight, but a multitude of stars lit the wide, grassy area between the tavern and the inn.

Partially obscured by the shadows, a masked figure hunched close to the tool shed toward the tavern's rear yard, watching as Barn and Arnie crossed the green.

If the concealed figure had taken a step away from the small building with its broken door, anyone happening to look in that direction would have seen its countenance courtesy of those same stars, but the figure in the shadows instinctively knew that, and remained as still as death.

"So far, we've had shit for luck together...are you sure you want to go through with this?" Arnie asked pointblank, as he and Barn strolled leisurely across the green, hands lightly clasped together.

Looking up, Barn asked, "Is this just cold feet, or are you trying to squirm out of marrying me?"

"No…sometimes I just feel afraid, I guess," Arnie confessed. "What if our best times are already behind us?" He started to laugh then, adding, "How much worse is it gonna get…that stuff sucked!"

"Let's put all that stuff to bed, and never wake it up again, OK?" Barn said. "None of it was ever because of us." He added encouragingly, "The bad times are behind us, babe."

Arnie stopped walking, and hugged his partner close to him with surprising force. "I know…I guess I just needed to hear it again."

"Don't worry about it," Barn said. Playfully, he added, "Besides, even if you did change your mind, the trip's not a complete waste of time…we got to see Whit Grissom."

"Ugly old bastard" Arnie said, laughing aloud as the partners resumed their walk.

"I'd hate to be in his shoes," Barn said. "Ugly as…what was it?"

"A barrel of boiled assholes," Arnie answered, as though it was a common description.

"Yeah, poor guy—ugly as a boiled asshole, smart as shit, and suffering from ED. How much worse can it get for him?"

"Lucky everything was OK for him in that department 25 years ago" Arnie joked, "or else the desperate woman still would be."

Barn laughed, as he walked contentedly along beside his partner. "Putting the infidelity aside, I felt bad for him...I mean, I hope you don't go around saying stuff like that about me in 30 or 40 years."

Arnie smiled in the starlight. "Don't worry about it, Peanut. You're way smarter than shit, and a lot better looking than a boiled asshole." Unable to keep a straight face any longer, Arnie stopped walking, and laughed.

"My self-esteem really kicked up a notch, Arnie. Thanks," Barn joked.

"No problem," Arnie chuckled.

Growing serious, Barn commented, "That was an interesting evening. Do you think Parker is dangerous, or was that just gossip...or an old woman's nerves, maybe?"

"I'm not sure" Arnie said, "but she doesn't seem, at least to me, like a woman who scares easily." Heaving a resigned sigh, he said, "We'll probably meet the girls at breakfast tomorrow."

"Can't see how we can help it," Barn commented.

"Right," Arnie said. "We'll just watch to see how Mr. Personality acts around 'em...I can't see us having to escort the girls all around town." He laughed, and added knowingly, "They probably wouldn't appreciate it too much anyway."

"Don't sell us short, Arnie" Barn laughed. "You've already seen some of the competition in Maple Grove Junction; gay or not, we're still gonna look like the best game in town."

As Arnie's laughter filled the green, and Barn automatically looked around to be sure they were not disturbing anyone, the shadowy figure near the shed slipped back into the woods, satisfied that the two men presented no threat.

> <

The tavern's vigorous owner shut off the lights, throwing the already dim interior of The White Star Tavern into pitch-blackness.

Heading back through the kitchen, where the narrow, closed-in staircase to the second floor was all but hidden by one of the tavern's two massive storage cabinets, the proprietress smiled; off season, while Whit regaled his assemblage of geezers with scintillating tales of his prostate, Gretchen often thought of climbing inside one of the cupboards, and remaining hidden until fall came around again.

After seeing his cronies off, Whit Grissom climbed the outside stairs to the tiny second floor apartment, with its ugly, avocado carpet and Mediterranean style furniture.

Performing his one act of physical activity for the day, the bad-tempered old man pulled the heavy curtains closed, and then, achieving his personal best, even managed to pick up two leaves that had dropped from the dusty, dried flower arrangement on the kitchen table.

When Gretchen entered the apartment from the hallway just minutes later, her heartthrob was already sitting on his ever-spreading backside, stuffing corn chips into his toothless maw.

Looking up when he heard his wife and meal ticket enter the room, he said, "Saw you talkin' to them two leaf peepers at the bar for a long time, woman."

"It's good that your damned eyes are still working, Whit, nothing else is," the feisty woman answered.

Looking at him with affection no one else in the world could understand, she said, "Those guys aren't leaf peepers—any jackass could see that."

"Don't matter what they is, Gretchen," Whit countered gruffly. "You shouldn't be tellin' folks 'bout George Parker, 'n how he beat his wife, or 'bout me cheatin' on ya'…they don't give a rat's ass, woman."

Ignoring her husband's latest assault on the English language, she said, "I worry when he's got women over there alone, Whit, you know I do. There are two over there now who aren't much more than grown girls…that little Lizzie's got the sweetest face…"

Whit shook his head, "I know, I know," he answered, cutting her off in mid-sentence. Changing the course of the conversation, he asked, "They got names, the two of 'em?"

Helping herself to the chair beside the couch where Whit was seated, she said, "Of course they have names, you damned fool…you think two women gave birth, and forgot to name what came out?"

Almost as soon as Gretchen took a seat, her husband switched to a reclining position on the sagging couch. "Ass tired from sitting all day, Whit?" she asked glibly.

Whit laughed at her quip, before answering her sarcastic question. "Nah" he replied, "no one's fool enough for that." He yawned, coughed and farted.

"You're a temple to vulgarity, Whit," Gretchen said with a smirk. Before Whit could comment, she answered, "Their names are Arnie Kotkin and Barney Moss."

Every night, their routine was the same, at least during peek leaf season. Whit, who had no interest in the answers at all, faithfully asked Gretchen about her barroom conversations.

She knew he could not have cared less, but she was always tickled that he made the effort to ask...at least he was making an effort to do something.

"Where're they from?" he queried, stuffing more chips into his mouth, and masticating them noisily.

"I don't remember 'em saying," Gretchen answered with a yawn. The long day was catching up to her, and she would soon make her way to their small bedroom, with its pale goldenrod paper and blue curtains.

Their bed, older than anything George Parker had in use over at the inn, once belonged to Gretchen's parents, as did the dresser and large, braided rug in the center of their room.

Sleeping on either of the latter items would probably have been more comfortable than sleeping on the former; the mattress was long overdue for replacement. Still, it was her nighttime sanctuary, and she was used to every lump and gully in its uneven surface.

Before she could say 'good night', Whit took one last opportunity to display the charm that won her heart. "Leaf peepers gotta be stupid, know it?" the fool on the couch said. "Gotta be livin' stuff to look at someplace, but they come troopin' up here to see dyin' leaves. I know stupid when I hear it, and that's stupid."

71

"I'm going to bed, old man," Gretchen said, thinking her Prince Charming had a nerve calling anyone else stupid. "Don't forget to shut out the lights."

Chapter 7

Even before he opened his eyes Monday morning, Barn was aware of rain beating against the windows.

Since childhood the energetic young man had found the sound of rain soothing at night, but rainy days did not fill him with the same sense of peace—especially on vacation.

Filled with watery, gray light the bedroom was a dismal chamber; it would have been a good morning to stay in bed, but he knew they could not do that. They had things to take care of today. He glanced at his watch; it was nearly 8:30.

"Arnie, wake up" he said, shaking his partner's shoulder gently.

"I don't feel like it, Barn...go back to sleep," Arnie mumbled.

Barn gave him a sharp jab in the ribs. "That's not what I want, Romeo," he said. "We have to go to the town hall today for the license."

Arnie grunted, "Later...we can even do it tomorrow." Making up his own requirements in a last-ditch effort to stay where he was, he added, "I think we've only gotta have that stuff something like 24 hours in advance. We've got time."

Rolling from his back onto his stomach, he pulled a pillow along with him, wrapping it around his ears as he moved.

"You look like a chicken wrap," Barn observed, but he would not be put off. Like a Chihuahua with a bone, he growled, "Come on. Get up, Arnie. It's almost 8:30, and breakfast is served at nine o'clock. We've gotta be out by 11:30." He gave his partner another shake—this time, there was nothing gentle about it.

Flipping over onto his back again, Arnie snapped, "That guy downstairs is a bastard. Christ, we're paying $72 a night for the damned room, but we can only be in it between 7:00 at night and 11:30 in the morning...and the bed's as comfortable as a pile of shit."

"I won't ask how you know that."

Still on his back, Arnie said, "He couldn't make it more obvious that he doesn't give a crap about the place...."

"Gretchen said it meant more to his wife than it does to him," Barn commented.

"Not much need for her to tell us, was there?" Arnie retorted. "Just look around! It's a nice house, but he's letting it go. What kind of business sense does that make? Even if he doesn't like it the way his wife did, he's still making money off of it…he should at least make a show of caring."

"Yeah" Barn replied, "but don't forget, he could be working someplace else part-time."

He looked at Arnie, who was raising an eyebrow, and elaborated, "Sometimes…what do they call 'em up here… innkeepers?"

"Good a word as any."

"Sometimes innkeepers probably can't make enough of a living to warrant giving up their day jobs entirely. They have their busy seasons, but I'll bet it's dead up here other times, even being just a few minutes off the highway…"

"I hadn't considered that," Arnie interjected, stretching out as though he might actually be comfortable.

"He pissed me off when we first got here" he stated flatly, "and Gretchen didn't make it any better telling us he beat his wife. I've gotta say I hate the guy, but you could be right about the part-time thing," the blond acknowledged, as his partner clambered out of bed.

Heading for the bathroom, Barn asked over his shoulder, "Could you toss my suitcase onto the foot of the bed for me, so I can get some underwear and socks?"

> <

Clad in his underwear, with a fresh T-shirt tossed over his shoulder, Barn vaulted onto the foot of the bed to pull his socks on.

"Take a look on the floor over there, would ya'?" he asked his already dressed partner. "I think my jeans are there."

Complying with the request, Arnie said, "Yes…right here." He picked them up, and tossed them to Barn.

"Need a hand with the T-shirt?" he asked gently.

He was coping better with it these days, but Arnie knew Barn still disliked asking for help—even if he needed it— so he always asked the question once. If the answer was 'no', he never followed it up with 'are you sure'.

"No, I can do it, babe," Barn replied. "This one's pretty stretched out."

He poked his left arm through the sleeve, and worked it up to his shoulder, before sticking his head and other arm in. Once he had wiggled into it, he hopped off the bed, and stuck his feet into his waiting sneakers.

Arnie led the way to the door. Turning the chipped, marble doorknob, he pondered, "I wonder what Mr. P serves for breakfast."

><

"Breakfast will be scrambled eggs, three sausage links, two slices of buttered rye toast, cranberry juice and coffee, with or without cream and sugar."

Known to the general public as George Parker, Mr. Personality did not take requests for substitutions, and he said so straight out.

With a voice that screeched like two pieces of rusty metal scraping together, he informed his visitors, "I serve only what I said I serve— nothing more, nothing less."

Barn watched the iron-haired 60ish man carefully as he laid out the morning repast for his guests. Parker never made eye contact with any of them, and he certainly did not smile or make small talk. The guy gave Barn the creeps; he might have given him the benefit of the doubt in front of Arnie up in their room, but Parker made him very uncomfortable.

In addition to Barn and Arnie, there were four other people staying at the little inn, and everyone was present for breakfast Monday morning. As Gretchen Grissom had told them last night, there were, in fact, three women there.

Two middle-aged people, undoubtedly siblings, for they looked very much alike, were seated opposite Barn and Arnie during breakfast, their backs to the smudged window overlooking the grassy parking area. Gretchen Grissom had called that one right too...the man had a face like thunder.

The woman, who clearly knew how to play the vacation chitchat game, introduced herself as Jane Slating, and explained that she and her brother, Sydney, were visiting Vermont from Burnham, Texas.

Trivial mealtime banter being a must in these types of places, she informed the group that she was a legal assistant, and Sydney was a lawyer; the JD in question chewed his toast, mindless of the introduction.

"Do you work for your brother?" Barn politely asked, buttering his toast and covering his scrambled eggs with pepper.

He really did not care whom Jane Slating worked for; he wanted to eat breakfast, and then head over to the town hall. Once that more important matter was taken care of, he thought maybe he and Arnie could take a nice drive someplace. It looked as though the sky would clear—it seemed to have stopped raining.

Jane took a sip of her light coffee, and then answered, "No, but I certainly know the job."

With a beaming smile that said she was proud of both herself and her brother, she added, "I work for real estate lawyers, which is what he is, but we're in two different firms."

Putting her cup gently down onto its saucer, she continued her opening remarks by informing everyone, "We got here on Saturday morning. We'll be here until next Saturday morning. We like to take a full week when we go places. We're planning to drive back as far as Connecticut, and then fly out of Bradley International. Coming up, we landed at Bradley and rented a car. We followed I-91 all the way up…it wasn't a bad drive at all. Very pretty scenery, and plenty of places to stop when we needed to."

Everyone at the long table smiled, and courteously feigned interest, with the exception of Jane's own brother.

A wiry, athletic-looking man, Sydney Slating, said indifferently, "I don't see the attraction. Leaves are leaves. What difference does the color make? I can't understand why all those idiots drive up to look at 'em…even if we don't have all the same trees in Texas as they've got up here, we've still got leaves."

He shot his sister an angry glance. He knew she was chattering on to disguise the fact that he was not speaking; her pleasant banter maddened him. He had come along on this trip only to get her to stop nagging him about all the fun they used to have when they traveled together years ago—before he met Eleanor.

Again, Jane tried to make her sibling look a bit less disagreeable, which was a Herculean undertaking these days.

"Sydney doesn't care for the cold," she explained, as though the disagreeable man were not sitting at her elbow. "I swear his teeth were chattering when he got back from his morning jog." She laughed pleasantly, adding, "The rain didn't help."

Arnie, with a forkful of overdone scrambled eggs midway to his mouth, and no real desire to have them finish the trip, said, "Barney and I are from New York. What's it…about 50 degrees this morning?"

Glancing at his partner in time to see him putting more pepper on the scorched eggs, he grinned; he wanted to tell him the eggs were beyond the help seasoning might give them.

The one-time science teacher continued, "Even with the rain earlier, I've been comfortable enough ever since I put my sweater on."

"When we left Texas—we're way down at the Mexican border—it was hot," Jane answered, pushing her own burned eggs around on the cracked plate they were served on. "I guess it's all a matter of what you're used to," she added with a light laugh.

The middle-aged woman was not blind to the fact that her brother did not even smile at her remark, while the others all did. She wished he would snap out of the funk he had been in since the divorce…the marriage was what had ruined his life; the dissolution of it gave him another shot at happiness. The still-pretty legal assistant could not understand why her brother failed to see it that way.

Jane Slating remembered a time when her brother had been laid-back and affable; his 12-year marriage to Eleanor Hopewell, whose father was CEO at the Dallas/Hopewell Oil Refinery, had sucked the life out of him.

The fiery-haired heiress had cheated on her husband repeatedly, leaving him a bitter man who found no humor in anything; he felt as though the entire world was in on a private joke, and he was the butt of it…and considering that she had slept with everyone from his one-time best friend to a senior partner at the office, he had good reason to feel that way.

Sydney Slating's sister worried that her once kind, jovial older brother had developed a neurosis about women.

He always seemed to be watching for character flaws in every woman he met, even if they did not exist, and Jane felt sure he was trying to convince himself that all women were like his ex-wife. It was not his fault that he had married a woman who had made a fool of him over and over again…they were all the same.

As she sat at the table that morning, Jane Slating could not shake the feeling that this was going to be a very long week.

The two young, single women Gretchen had spoken of rounded out the guest list.

The ultra thin Gloria Baines, whose long red tresses hung limply around her thin face, told the assembled guests that she worked at a bank near her home in Bryant, Maryland, while her friend, Lizzie Tidman, golden-haired and blessed with features as sweet as the Christ child's, informed the others that she was a receptionist at Perkton's Hair Salon, also located in Bryant.

The women explained that they had met at Lizzie's workplace, and became friends quickly.

The obviously good-natured Lizzie joked, "God didn't give Glo that auburn hair, but He helped her find a friend who could get her a color appointment fast."

Cheerily she added, "Her real reason for wanting to come to Vermont was to check out the colors of the leaves; she's looking to see if there's anything she likes better than Perkton's #267."

Although the young women said their primary reason for vacationing in Vermont was to enjoy the scenery, and bring home plenty of pictures, they also professed a desire to have a bit of fun, and maybe find a cute guy or two.

From her seat at the head of the table, Lizzie announced, "We've found the scenery...the leaves are gorgeous, and we've taken, like, a million pictures..."

Her red-haired traveling companion tossed in, "But finding fun's been tricky. The tavern lady told us there's a movie here someplace, but we haven't been there yet."

Giggling, she poked fun at her vacation destination by saying, "There's no sense doing everything in the first couple days."

The receptionist's deep green eyes flashed, as she resumed speaking. "If you think it's hard to find fun here, try to find a man who's not halfway to dead."

As her friend aimed her own jest at the male population of Maple Grove Junction, Gloria was openly eyeing the young male population at the table. She thought the little guy with the huge, dark eyes was cute.

Speaking to the group at large, but looking directly at Barn, she giggled again, as she explained, "We've been here since Thursday night, but all the men we've seen up until now make the hills look young…and they've been married for a thousand years."

Her giggles were charming, even if she was not entirely right on that point.

Whit Grissom was already married, although not for a thousand years, but his three toothless friends were all single, and every one of them would have been considered a catch—about 40 years ago—especially Myles Buck. His service station had always turned a nice profit.

"So what else have you girls done so far?" Jane Slating asked. She had given up all hope of finding anything salvageable among the scorched mound of eggs on her plate; like her brother, she was chewing on toast.

"What do you care, Jane?" Sydney drawled waspishly, beating a piece of toast down to crumbs while he buttered it.

Annoyed with his sister, the inn, everyone at the table and his life at large, Sydney abruptly brushed the crumbs onto the floor, and put his knife down.

As far as he was concerned, this meal was filled with all the rollicking gaiety of the Last Supper, and he wanted it to end. Anything would be better than to sit among strangers eating the crap George Parker put on their plates.

Taken aback by her brother's rudeness, Jane did not answer for a few seconds. When she did speak, it was to say, "People on vacation do make small talk, Sydney. You used to do it yourself. Honestly, I can't understand why you are letting this thing ruin your entire life…"

Before the very surprised guests at the table could learn more about this 'thing' that was destroying Sydney's life, he commanded, "Shut up, Jane!" His voice, although as cold as death, did nothing to cool the white-hot temper blazing in his eyes. Sydney Slating seemed like a force to be reckoned with.

While Jane Slating sat staring at her brother in open-mouthed amazement, Lizzie awkwardly tried to get back to a friendly topic.

Answering the question that had been directed to her friend at the end of the table, she said, "We found some antique shops...our guide book said there were, like, a million. We've checked out quite a few, and done a lot of sleeping in."

Again, Sydney sprang into action, pouncing on the innocent remark.

"So that's why we haven't seen you before," he snarled. "If we didn't see your car in the lot, and sometimes notice it was gone, we wouldn't even know you were here."

The lawyer's voice, which somehow managed to convey callous indifference and righteous anger at once, was also oddly accusatory.

A gentle girl from a quiet family, Lizzie was unaccustomed to dealing with the obvious rage being tossed her way. Even as she looked down the length of the table for backup from Gloria, she defended their actions by saying, "We've been too tired to make it to breakfast until now."

Never one to defend when she could attack, Gloria stared into Sydney Slating's eyes until he looked away; the devil would have flinched under scrutiny like that. Clearly enjoying his discomfort, she asked, "Are you in the habit of watching other people's cars, Mr. Slating?"

Before Sydney could make himself look even worse, Jane asked the young women if they had been born in Maryland.

Without taking her eyes away from Jane's brother, Gloria answered, "Yes, I was born there."

Lizzie quickly responded, "My mother lived in Vermont a long time ago, but by the time I was born, the family had moved to Maryland. I'm glad to be able to see it for myself; I've never been here before."

As she sipped more coffee, and hoped her brother would keep his mouth shut, Jane said, "Oh, how nice…kind of a homecoming."

After all she had witnessed in their short time at the breakfast table this morning, Jane knew this vacation was anything but nice, but it seemed like the right thing to say.

She hoped the girls would forget about her brother's bad manners, and enjoy their day. She had noticed Gloria making puppy eyes at the dark-haired young man at the table, and thought that Lizzie and the other young man would probably be paired off by the end of the day whether they wanted to be or not.

Barn looked out through the dirty, mullioned window behind the Slating siblings as he forced down his peppery eggs, and listened to the other guests.

Finally seeing the opportunity to rejoin the conversation with a casual comment, he announced, "Ladies, the sun's coming out. You'll be able to take some more pictures, today, too."

Arnie reached for another piece of tasteless toast, while forcing himself to joke, "If you girls are seriously looking for guys, there must be more of 'em in Maryland than there are up here…younger ones, anyway."

Gloria replied, "The men in Bryant are all political types, lawyers and all—very boring. I like kind of outdoorsy-looking guys, and Lizzie does too."

Gloria also liked her outdoorsy types little, and Barn fit the bill. She favored him with a playful smile and a come-and-get-it look.

Catching the amorous look shot his way by the obviously hot-to-trot redhead, Barn shivered inwardly. He should have known the rain beating on the window this morning was a bad omen.

"What are you guys doing after breakfast?" Gloria eagerly asked, her bright blue eyes boring directly into Barn's nearly black ones.

Seeing the light of salvation at the end of the tunnel of love Gloria had hastily constructed, her intended beau answered truthfully, "Going for a marriage license…we're getting married on Wednesday."

Sydney Slating choked on his rye toast.

Chapter 8

Red hair billowing out behind her as she hustled across the grassy parking lot, Gloria Baines called out, "Hey, wait up, guys. I've gotta talk to you." Glancing back over her shoulder she yelled, "Come on, Lizzie, hurry up!"

Now wearing her blond hair in a neat chignon at the base of her neck, Lizzie Tidman was standing near the inn's double doors looking toward their rented Honda. Not knowing what her friend was up to, she walked slowly across the grassy parking lot.

The two men stopped at the sound of Gloria's cry, one on either side of Barn's car, and waited while Gloria, brandishing her scarf in one hand and camera in the other, drew up to them.

"I'm really sorry," she said. "I had no idea...I would never have put someone on the spot like that."

As she spoke, she slung her camera around her neck, and casually tied the paisley print scarf around her head, knotting the ends at the back, beneath her hair.

It was not a good look for her.

"It's OK, don't worry about it," Barn said.

The apology made and accepted, he was ready to get going. Reaching to open his car door, he grinned; Gretchen Grissom pegged another one exactly right. Gloria did look funny with that thing on her head. The babushka could not be forced at gunpoint to go with the redhead's green-and-white striped sweater and nearly neon lime slacks.

"Lizzie and I would like to tag along," the young woman announced unexpectedly.

Her blue eyes took in the color of Barn's Toyota—clearly she thought flashy red topped tedious tan any day.

"We'll get your stuff done first, and then you can drive us to a few of the antique shops. How's that?" Giving Barn no time to answer, she plowed on, "We'd like to take some more pictures today too, and stop to eat of course."

The men exchanged glances over the top of the car. The woman speaking to them had gone from apologetic to pushy in what had to be record time. Arnie raised a quizzical eyebrow; he was not thrilled about the prospect of having uninvited guests, but in a move his wishy-washy father would have applauded, he was putting the question to Barn.

Across the car, Arnie's partner, who had opened his mouth to say, 'I don't think so' suddenly found himself spitefully saying, "Hop in, Gloria. Arnie, reach in, and unlock that door for her, would ya'?"

The scorching look he shot across the roof of his car could have melted the polar ice cap, had it been directed that way. Not only was this not how he had envisioned the day, but now his partner was acting like his kind, but weak-willed, adoptive father. He felt his blood pressure kick up a notch.

Furious himself, Arnie unlocked the rear door, and held it while the redhead climbed in. He closed the back door much harder than was necessary, and did the same thing to his own door when he got in.

Mad about the dirty trick Barn had just pulled, Arnie knew he was more incensed by his own behavior.

He knew he should have been man enough to tell the pushy redhead 'no' in the first place…he had known that was what Barn was ready to say, but he had clearly given his partner a look that said it was his call.

Arnie saw the resemblance to his adoptive father, and knew Barn had seen it too.

Already behind the wheel when his partner took possession of the passenger seat, Barn glared at him, and clearly mouthed the words, "You'll say 'no' the next time." Sticking the knife of his anger all the way in, he deliberately mouthed the name 'Joseph'.

Angry and embarrassed, Arnie gave him the finger, and mouthed back, "Damned right I will."

If the probate judge had suddenly materialized in the front seat at that point asking them to say 'I do', both would have squashed him like an unfortunate spider.

In the backseat, Gloria was paying no attention to her unwilling hosts' brief, hot and soundless exchange; she was sticking her head out the door to yell at her dawdling friend.

"Come on!" she called out in an authoritative voice. "I told the guys we'd go with them—get a move on."

Lizzie did not hasten her step; she walked up to the car, clearly wondering how this situation arose. "I thought we were going antiquing," she said.

From the backseat, Gloria snapped, "We are, but we're riding with the guys first." Adopting a more pleasant voice, she sweetly added, "It'll be fun, Liz—come on, don't be a spoilsport."

Lizzie shook her head, wondering what Gloria Baines had in mind. Why tag along with a gay couple on their way to get a marriage license?

Looking out his window at precisely that moment, Barn saw the woman's expression, and mistook it for embarrassment. Offering her a sympathetic smile, he said, "It's OK, Lizzie, we don't mind. Hop in." He reached back to unlock the rear door for her.

"You need a new car, Barn…something with locks you can work from the front seat," Arnie grumbled, redirecting his embarrassed anger at himself toward something concrete.

"So buy me one," Barn shot back.

"Buy it yourself. I might need to ask for your opinion." Arnie knew he was the one in the wrong, but he was too mad at himself to give in yet.

"You didn't just ask for my opinion," Barn answered snottily.

As Lizzie climbed unenthusiastically into the backseat, her red-haired traveling companion, totally oblivious to the fact that a quarrel was underway in the front seat, said, "When you're done talking about new cars, let's get going. Do you know where the town hall is?"

Too mad to be civil to anyone at that point, Barn just made an affirmative-sounding grunt, and started the car.

"OK, then," Gloria said, her voice sugary, "Liz and I'll wait in the car, while you guys do what you need to." Blue eyes shining in her friend's direction, she cheerily added, "We can always find something to gossip about, right Lizzie?"

The neatly coiffed woman beside her made no comment.

> <

In the shadowy hallway outside the Town Clerk's office, Barn whispered, "Before we go in…um…I'm sorry about that stuff in the car, Arnie. I shouldn't have gotten so mad, but stop acting like Mr. K, all right? You've already proven you're no one's patsy. Why didn't you just tell her 'no'?"

Arnie shook his head and, with obvious confusion, admitted, "I don't know…it's the first time in my life I've ever acted like Pop—spineless, ya' know?"

Wearing a self-conscious smile, he truthfully admitted, "You got pissed off, and I don't blame you. It was my fault. You said what you said, because I acted the way I did."

"It's just that it's not the way I wanted the day to be," Barn answered. His midnight brown eyes were fixed intently on his partner's face as he explained, "I had this picture of us going for the marriage license, and then just spending a nice day together. Gloria Baines was nowhere in the plans."

Relieved now that he had admitted his fault and apologized, Arnie smiled and said, "Jeez, she's something, isn't she?"

"Yeah, but what?" Barn queried, his own resentment now pushed aside. "One minute she's friendly enough, and the next minute she's like...um...I hate to say this, but she's like your mother used to be—maybe that's why you acted like Mr. K."

With a puzzled shake of his dark head, he added, "I keep wondering why Gretchen said Gloria was nice enough..."

Arnie cut in, "Maybe 'nice enough' is her euphemism for 'bitchy'." With a wink, he added, "For the record, my mother dresses a lot better."

Barn smiled, and then asked, "We're OK, babe? No more hard feelings?"

"No more hard feelings" Arnie replied, bending to give the other man a gentle kiss.

Barn grinned up at him, "Are you gonna buy me a new car?"

Grasping his life partner's hand as they entered the small office, Arnie answered, "We'll see."

> <

Marriage license procured, the partners walked leisurely back to the car, where the women gossiped in the backseat, hands flying like caged birds.

Barn was paying no attention to the women in the backseat of his car as they approached it, but his partner was. Giving a quick nod toward the wildly gesticulating women, Arnie said, "I wonder what they're talking about."

"Who cares?" Barn said, clearly uninterested.

Laughing vociferously, Arnie said, "Look at 'em, Barn. Either it's really hot gossip, or they're swinging at flies."

Curious because of his partner's highly amused reaction, Barn focused his eyes on the occupants of the Toyota's backseat; they did look funny.

"From the way they're flinging their hands all around" Barn chuckled, "I'd say it's not 'what' they're talking about, it's 'whom'. I think someone's getting raked over the coals."

No sooner had the couple reached the parked car, and opened their doors than Gloria chirped, "Back so soon?" With no answer being necessary, since, obviously, they were back, she continued, "We've just been laughing at how quickly the weather changes."

"Yeah…it does" Barn said, hoping weather was not going to be the major topic of the day, yet appreciating that it was not an argumentative comment.

Gloria continued her mindless prattle, "I've heard people say, we both have, that if you don't like the weather in New England, you just have to wait five minutes. We didn't know it was really true. How do these people ever know how to dress?"

She giggled merrily, and needlessly added, "It was miserable this morning, but it's beautiful now...we've got our cameras all ready."

"Pictures or antique shops first?" Arnie asked the girls, pulling his seat belt on. Like his partner, he hoped the conversation was going to improve. If they gestured like that over the weather, he could hardly wait for world politics to be discussed.

"Get it OK?" Lizzie asked from the backseat.

"Yeah, fine," Barn answered. Lizzie seemed like a decent sort of woman to him; friends could have such different personalities he thought.

"When's the ceremony?" Lizzie asked, genuinely interested.

Barn replied, "Wednesday at two o'clock..."

Gloria cut him off. "Let's head for the shops. We can stop to take pictures along the way, if we feel like it...or on the way back. You didn't have any other plans."

Fingers clutching the wheel so tightly that his knuckles were white, Barn asked, "Which way, Gloria?" Amazed by the way she had just brushed their conversation aside, he looked over his right shoulder to catch a glimpse of the redhead seated behind Arnie.

"It's really easy, just follow the road that way," Gloria explained, paying no attention to the driver's obviously annoyed expression. She pointed down the road in the direction of her choice. "It's less than a mile."

Lizzie added meekly, "It's the road we took yesterday."

The redhead mocked, "Lizzie blew right by the first place we got to. How's that for stupid? Not another damned thing up here to look at but leaves, and she missed a building... it'll be on your left."

As Barn started the car, he said, "It's not stupid, Gloria. It could happen to anyone—don't feel bad, Lizzie."

It was obvious that Gloria's blatantly tasteless remark hurt Lizzie's feelings, and he openly offered his support. Silently, he wondered how Gloria Baines talked to people she hated.

Lizzie responded softly, "Thank you, Barney."

After those three words, she remained silent until they reached the first antique shop.

Chapter 9

Located in the tiny widening of the road that was the town of Green River, Vermont, the musty little repository for things from another time was appropriately, if predictably, named 'Green River Antiques'. According to the hand-lettered sign in the dusty window, the little shop claimed to specialize in vintage clothing.

Studying the placard for a moment as they stood before the shop, Arnie inquired of the small group, "Does that mean they're probably clothes our grandparents wore?"

"Get hold of yourself, babe" Barn laughed, reaching to open the door. "I'd suspect your grandparents wouldn't have been caught dead wearing the stuff in this shop."

Following their tiny leader into the store, both women smiled, but it was Gloria who brazenly asked, "How much money do you come from, Arnie?"

"Enough," Arnie said coolly. He was not angered by the fact that his partner had alluded to familial wealth, but he resented Gloria's blunt question.

"Oops," Gloria said. "Sorry…didn't mean to pry."

"Yes you did," Arnie muttered under his breath; the constant flip-flop of Gloria's personality was getting on his nerves. His partner's quickly flashed thumbs-up made him feel better, and he let the matter drop.

When the foursome entered the little shop, they found that, aside from the owner, who lowered his paper to watch them from behind a glass counter at the front of the store, the shop was devoid of life.

The girls poked slowly through the center of the store, and eventually made their way to the right hand side.

Walking slowly toward the other side of the store, Barn and Arnie could hear the creaking of the owner's chair as he turned from one side to the other, trying to keep an eye on everyone.

"Must be a lot of shoplifting among the vintage get-ups crowd," Barn whispered to his partner.

"Vintage clothing, not vintage get-ups," Arnie corrected him, pseudo serious.

Stopping beside a rack of old coats, he pulled a slightly faded navy blue jacket out, and held it up for Barn's inspection. "Can you see Melvin Fine in this?" he joked, rolling his eyes as he thought of his deceased maternal grandfather.

"Yeah, sure…he wore it the day before he wore this one." Chuckling as he extracted a battered herringbone coat from among the others, Barn added, "He probably had this one on when he was drafting the trust fund for you and your brothers."

Arnie smirked, "You're bad, Barney."

Growing somber then, the blond man whispered, "I never thought I'd be the only one here to enjoy it…"

"I'm sorry, babe" Barn said, putting one hand on his partner's forearm. "I didn't mean to make you feel bad; I wasn't thinking."

Shaking his head of tawny curls, Arnie protested, "It's OK…I know you didn't. It just got me thinking again, that's all." He smiled weakly, saying, "Jim's having a ball with his share while he's in the…ah…hospital, and Jerry won't have the chance to blow his share on stupid stuff."

He hung the once dark blue jacket back up, and looked idly through the rack at the other coats before turning to peruse the shop with his eyes.

Barn patted his arm again in a consoling way. "Just remember what we talked about on the way up," he said gently. "The baby's being taken care of."

"I remember it every day," Arnie answered.

Now leaning against the coat rack while he looked around the shop, he noticed that the girls had gone about three-quarters of the way to the rear of the store, and the owner, apparently satisfied that they were not criminals here to steal his inventory of ancient clothing, had returned to his paper.

Barn followed his friend's lead and hung up the herringbone coat he had been pointlessly holding onto. Surprisingly, a tweed jacket caught his eye, and he pulled it out. "This isn't bad," he commented, studying it more closely.

"Your poor parents worked two jobs when you were little so they wouldn't be dressing you out of a rag box, and here you are looking at coats somebody probably died in."

The shorter man grinned, and hung the jacket back with the others.

> <

While the two men whispered confidentially among the coats, Lizzie wandered away from Gloria, and headed toward a counter set against the store's rear wall.

The antediluvian glass cabinet housed a plethora of jewelry, dishes and small gadgets; many pieces, like the dishes, were on top of the cabinet.

Lizzie recognized a meat grinder that was still in use in her mother's kitchen, and was taking a closer look at it when Arnie and Barn walked over to her.

"Find anything?" Barn asked.

Before Lizzie could answer, Gloria strode up beside the other young woman, and said, "Oh, look, Depression glass. Doesn't your mother have a set like that?"

"She has more...she's got the service pieces," Lizzie answered turning away from the meat grinder, to look over at the dishes.

Gloria turned a plate over. "Look at that" she said, "$37.50!" She put the dish back into the display with the other pieces, and said, "Wait 'til you tell her she's eating off valuable antiques."

Lizzie shrugged, and then said, "Maybe we should just have sold them...the meat grinder too. They want $65 for that."

She moved down the counter to look at the jewelry, and a particularly pretty string of pearls caught her eye. Taking a look at the small white tag attached to the string of lustrous little orbs, she exclaimed, "Whew! Way to rich for me."

"How much are they?" Gloria asked.

"$165...I thought maybe they'd be $20 or so."

"I'll get them for you, if you'd like," Gloria offered, her voice just a shade too sweet.

Lizzie grimaced. Shaking her blond head, she said, "No, thanks." In a sarcastic timbre, she added, "You've done enough already."

Barn and Arnie walked away; neither one wanted to listen to round two of the women's bitch fest.

They wasted no time walking back up the aisle they had just come down, and headed toward the front of the store. "Let 'em battle it out back there," Barn said. "We heard enough in the car before."

If the young men had looked around, they would have seen Lizzie start to follow them, and been surprised by the forcefulness with which Gloria grabbed her arm.

It was doubtful that they would have heard the words the redhead whispered. "Liz, I pushed too far before," she said. "I shouldn't have insinuated you were stupid."

A hint of a cat-like smile played around the corners of her well-shaped mouth, as she added, "You're not stupid; you're smart enough to know a good deal..."

In an equally soft whisper, the blond receptionist interjected, "When this is over..."

It was the redhead's turn to interrupt. Her voice brusque, but still a whisper, she said, "When this is over, Lizzie, you'll see that it was worth it...chill out before you blow it."

> <

After visiting several more of the area's enticing little antiques shops and taking pictures of each and every one of them, the band of tourists stopped for lunch in Falling Rock Junction, a town that made Green River look like a booming metropolis.

Gloria had no trouble framing the entire downtown area in her camera's viewfinder.

The center of Falling Rock Junction boasted only three buildings—each one smaller than the one before it: an IGA Market; a hole-in-the-wall eatery, whose name matched its menu, 'Sandwiches'; and a one-pump service station, whose owner was sitting on the front steps of his ramshackle office.

Customers could only drive onto the service station's property; parking for the market and the restaurant was apparently 'find it if you can' on the narrow street—judging by today, finding a prime spot was never a problem.

Barn parked his car in front of the cafe, and the hungry travelers disembarked.

Heading for the humble sandwich shop, all four members of the group were surprised to see the service station's owner get up from his perch on the rickety stairs, and walk toward the shop; apparently, the man was a small business entrepreneur.

Running his hands down the front of his faded blue overalls, the man, who sported a thick mustache, wore a tattered baseball cap over his gray curls, its brim shielding his eyes from the sun. His cheeks were weathered; no sunscreen ever covered that skin.

"Nice day, ain't it folks?" he called out to them.

"Yeah…very nice," Barn answered for the foursome.

"Wantin' some lunch, are ya'?" the gas station attendant turned restaurateur asked.

"Ah…yeah…I guess," Barn said tentatively, glancing first at his watch, and then looking toward his fellow travelers for help.

No one spoke; no one was going to toss out any other excuse for their presence here—using the bathroom, asking for direction, or maybe just wanting to have their picture taken in front of Falling Rock Junction's entire metropolitan area.

"Well, come on in, then, kids" the old man instructed them. "I got baloney today."

He said 'baloney' so proudly that one might have suspected the lunchmeat was a more choice cut of meat than prime rib.

Entering the eatery, and taking seats at the quaint yellow counter, the four city dwellers were amused by the simple menu on the wall:

Sandwiches: IGA cold cuts;

Soda: IGA Cola;

Coffee: IGA regular/decaf;

Snacks: IGA Potato chips and sugar cookies.

"Nice that he patronizes the local grocery store," Barn whispered to his partner.

Arnie whispered back, "He probably runs that too."

Barn stifled a laugh, but only momentarily; it broke free when their host asked what they wanted to eat, and Lizzie glanced around, as though there was another menu written on another wall.

"Sandwiches and chips will be fine," Arnie said, ignoring Lizzie's double take, and Barn's guffaws. He added, "My treat."

The old man behind the counter smiled; he had no idea what his four young customers where laughing about, but they seemed harmless enough. Thinking it was just a matter of the little guy and the pretty blond girl having the hots for each other, he continued to play the good host.

"Chips are right there in that basket," he explained, pointing to a large woven basket that none of his customers had noticed yet; it was at the far end of the counter.

After giving those simple instructions, he headed over to a small refrigerator behind the counter; today's special was already wrapped and ready to go.

He extracted four sandwiches, and placed them on the counter before turning back to collect four cans of cola.

The two women watched the old man go about his work, but Barn paid no attention; he was busy razzing his partner. "You're so generous, Arnie. Are you paying for the soda too, or are you a little short on funds this month?"

Arnie laughed at the good-natured teasing, and then responded, "I'll spring for the soda, but if you want coffee afterwards, you're on your own."

"If anyone wants coffee after their meal, I'll get it," Lizzie said with a big smile, pulling a $5 bill from her jeans pocket.

"Cookies too," she said as an afterthought, as she counted the change she had just fished out of another pocket.

Paying very little attention to what the others were saying, Gloria said, "I think we should head back after this. We still want to take some pictures; there're some really pretty spots on the road heading back to the inn."

Chapter 10

"I love the curtains I picked up," Lizzie commented as Barn set a course for the inn.

She was growing nervous, and trying to keep up the appearance of making small talk was getting to be a strain. She wished the day were over, as she chattered robotically, "Lace is so much nicer in a bedroom, at least I think it is, than something heavier."

With her small package resting on her knees, she settled back in her seat, feeling the involuntary tremors in her arms and legs.

"Which shop did you get them in?" Gloria asked, forcing the other woman to keep talking.

Lizzie shrugged, and said, "I don't remember the name… but they were right in my price range—loose change to $5."

She dug an already crumbled receipt out of her pocket, and read from it, "$3.25."

"You and I shop the same way, Lizzie," Barn commented, eyes on the narrow, twisting road. "If it's cheap enough, I'll get it, but Arnie approaches shopping from the other angle. If we don't need to re-mortgage the condo, it's probably not worth having."

Laughing heartily, Arnie said, "I'm getting better about that…one day last week, I caught myself buying paper plates."

"You were probably trying to get on my good side," Barn joked.

"Paper plates are all it takes?" Lizzie asked, feeling relieved that the guys had joined the conversation; it took the pressure off of her.

From the front seat, Arnie chortled, "Barn's always been easy."

> <

The dusk of early fall was closing in by the time the foursome arrived back in Maple Grove Junction at 6:30.

Passing the tavern, they saw Gretchen Grissom, her sturdy figure illuminated by the yellowish light from the open door behind her.

She waved to them as they circled the green, and went into her neighbor's small parking lot.

Barn pulled into one of the least grassy spaces, and then, leaving Lizzie's curtains in the car, the four young people walked back across the green.

As they drew nearer to the tavern, the old woman called out to them, "Come on in. The old bastard and his three cronies haven't started in on the meat yet. Have a roast beef sandwich before they get it."

Everyone followed her into the crowded tavern where, even at that early hour, the tables were all filled. There were a few seats left at the bar, and Gloria and Lizzie made straight for them.

Barn and Arnie followed them, taking the last two available seats in the place.

"Buds and sandwiches all 'round?" Gretchen queried, already drawing off the malts.

"Sounds good," the four young patrons said together.

Drumming her fingers on the bar, Lizzie asked, "Exactly where is the movie theater, Mrs. Grissom?" before the older woman could step into the back room to make their sandwiches.

Gretchen looked back at the pretty blond and explained, "The movie house is straight down the road a piece, about a mile north of here. Show times are 8:15 and 10:45."

With a kindly smile, the old woman asked, "What's got you so jittery tonight, Lizzie?"

"Nothing…sorry" Lizzie answered, clapping one hand over the other—she had been drumming her fingers so fast her hands should have cramped up.

Anticipating the next question, the old woman informed the foursome, "I'm not sure what they're showing… probably still that thing with the guy who takes God's job for a week. Picture's OK, and the theater makes decent popcorn, too…real butter. Up here, watching 'em make it passes for entertainment—especially in the winter."

After Gretchen had disappeared into the kitchen, Lizzie asked woodenly, "Wanna go? We've got plenty of time to eat and still be there for the 8:15 show."

Barn wrinkled his nose. "Not really. I'm tired. I think I'll head over to the room after we eat, take a shower, and crash for the night. Don't let me stop the rest of you."

Taking a swig of the beer Gretchen had placed in front of him, Arnie said, "I don't remember the last time I went to the movies…are you sure you don't mind if I go, Barn?"

Barn shook his head, "No...go on. Like I said, I'm just gonna eat, maybe have a couple beers, and go back to the room."

"Glo, are you in?" Lizzie asked.

The redhead answered, "No thanks, I'm not in the mood for that much excitement tonight. You guys go ahead. I'm gonna stick around here for a little while...a couple beers sound pretty good to me, too."

> <

At their customary table near the fireplace, Whit Grissom and his buddies were entertaining a new guest. Finding himself without beer in the refrigerator for the first time in a year, George Parker had strolled across the green to bum a brew off of his neighbors.

Ignoring Gretchen, whom he disliked as much as she disliked him, Parker had made his way to the back table; he claimed no great love for Whit, but Myles Buck was his friend, and he had nothing against the retired cousins either.

All things considered, the five old men were enjoying themselves playing poker, drinking beer and watching the crowd.

Parker was surprised to see the young foursome enter the tavern just as he looked up.

Sundry visions of perverted pleasures of the flesh leapt to the forefront of the innkeeper's mind, as he inconspicuously whispered to his old friend and service station boss, "Wish I could've spent the day as a fly."

"How's that?" a puzzled Myles whispered back, raising his beer mug to his mouth to disguise the movement of his lips, not that anyone was looking—even their tablemates were paying no attention, busy as they were with the 'drinking beer' part of their evening's entertainment.

Nodding his ugly head toward the bar, Parker said, "See those two babes up there...Blondie and the redhead?"

"A'ya," Myles responded, even though they really were not standing close enough for him to make out their features.

With an obscene snort, Parker explained, "They're staying at my place...the men too. Thing is, they're queerer than $3 bills. I'll bet whatever they did today ain't been pretty."

The hands wrapped around his beer mug twitched; he wished he could have gotten a real look at the imagined scene his mind was dangling before him.

Before turning their full attention back to their own grueling agenda for the evening, the two men shared a laugh that was both obscene and embarrassed; Myles Buck was not sure if his part-time employee was hosting one pair of $3 bills over at the inn or two, so he laughed to save face.

When the two blonds, male and female, left together sometime later, Parker gave Myles a punch in the arm, and said snidely, "Can't think why they're pairing off that way."

Sure that at least one of the two young people heading for the tavern's wide doorway was gay, Myles Buck felt safe in saying, "Hardly seems any point."

George reached over to give his friend, boss and future landlord a powerful clap on the back; both men laughed heartily.

Continuing to watch Barn and Gloria, George immediately noticed when Barn got up a short time later, dropped some bills on the bar, and headed for the door. "Look, Myles" he said urgently, "the little guy's going too…"

Myles was on a roll now. "A threesome," he chortled obscenely. "Makes ya' wonder which one's gonna be in the middle, don't it?"

> <

"What time is it?" Barn asked drowsily, rolling from his stomach onto his back and knuckling his eyes.

Arnie was crawling into bed, and his added weight on the lumpy mattress was enough to disturb him; it was also enough to get the broken mattress springs moving, and several new lumps materialized.

"Exactly 11:11" Arnie answered, taking a quick look at the four red vertical lines on the digital clock.

After giving his pillow a few thumps in the vain hope of softening it, he plopped down on his back before asking, "Anyone stop by?" His huge, teasing grin was wasted on the thick darkness blanketing the room, but Barn could hear the mirth in his voice.

"Yeah, sure," he joked back easily. "George came up for a quick romp, but he left about half an hour ago…you only just missed Sydney by a couple minutes."

While Arnie enjoyed the joke, his tiny partner yawned, and then asked, "How was the movie?"

"It was good…kind of funny," Arnie answered.

Without being asked, he offered his critique of the snack food. "The popcorn was good. Gretchen was right…real butter. Before the movie started, we stood in the lobby for a little while, and watched it pop."

Squiggling over to escape a bedspring that was now poking him in the back, Barn commented, "That's scary, babe."

With a short chuckle, Arnie answered, "No, what's scary is that we weren't the only people watching it…every single person who came in stood there watching those damned kernels like they were what we paid our six bucks to see."

The bed shook with laughter, as Barn said, "Maybe it was more entertaining than watching the coming attractions— they probably get about three movies up here in the course of six years."

Continuing to mock the evening he had just spent, Arnie said, "I'm not kidding ya', Barn. Lizzie and I were the first people to go inside and take seats…the rest of 'em stayed in the lobby watching the popcorn until just before the movie started."

Still giggling, Barn rolled onto his side, and cuddled against his popcorn-watching friend. He closed his eyes, as his partner's strong arms encircled his tiny waist, and immediately drifted off to sleep.

"You staying awake, or going back to sleep?" the willowy blond asked, pressing his lips gently against Barn's thick, dark hair.

Barn snored his response.

> <

Lizzie Tidman opened the door, and stepped quietly into her room before pushing her key back into her pocket. Except for Gloria's shallow breathing and the hammering of her own heart, all was still.

With her fingers trembling, the fair-haired woman undressed and crawled into her own bed—the twin to the one Gloria slumbered in, her conscience untroubled by what she had done that night.

Lizzie considered setting the alarm clock, but decided against it. Tonight, she really was tired; if she missed breakfast in the morning, she missed it.

She knew that the deed was done, and she felt like she had no life left in her.

> <

The door slammed back against the wall with such force that the doorknob gouged a hole in the drywall.

The lone figure in the apartment leapt up, spilling beer onto the carpet.

"You scared the heart outta me…"

The enraged voice of the newcomer said, "We've gotta talk."

Chapter 11

Barely distinguishable from the darkness enveloping it like a velvet shroud, the figure crept soundlessly up the stairs to the second floor.

Familiar with the layout of the rooms, the pseudo phantom moved surreptitiously toward the door, and bent to slide a scrap of paper beneath it.

Straightening slowly—sense of hearing on red alert—the intruder listened to the weighty quiet of the midnight hour. Was the house whispering something…maybe asking what the interloper was doing there?

Never given to fancy before, the prowler dismissed the whimsical notion, and headed for the stairs again—it was just the sound of an old house settling.

The uninvited guest left silently, knowing a return trip would take place in just a few hours more.

> <

"All right, Barn?" Arnie whispered, his breath on his partner's face as soft as the breeze from the flapping wings of a butterfly.

It was still early, 7:19 by the digital clock on the rickety nightstand, but a ray of indigo tinted light found its way around the ragged edge of the window shade and through the curtains.

"Umm?" was the sleepy reply from the small body nestled beside him.

Arnie stretched his long limbs, yawning with gusto, as he repeated, "I said I'm gonna take a shower…all right? Did you wanna join me?" He crawled out of the big, uncomfortable bed, and pulled the down comforter off of his reluctant-to-awaken friend.

Even sleepy, the other man's reflexes were good; he grabbed one corner of the comforter, and tugged it back up over his pillow-tussled hair.

"No thanks…I took one last night, while you were out watching popcorn," he answered.

Arnie chuckled softly, as he gathered up his clothes and padded toward the bathroom door; his partner was snoring again before he stepped inside.

> <

In the other room overlooking the inn's front yard, Lizzie Tidman stood under the shower's hot spray scrubbing her body and hair as though the act of physically cleansing herself would clear away the deceit she had let herself become a part of; no good could come of the plan, she had known it from the outset, but her mother needed the financial help desperately.

Without warning, her thoughts were disturbed as the shower door first shook with the force of an angry rap, and an instant later, was pulled back with such surprising force that Lizzie grabbed a built-in handrail on the side of the shower stall for support. Her hands closed around it none too soon—her feet were already slipping.

Gloria Baines stuck her head in, her long, auburn tresses catching some of the shower's spray.

Ignoring her friend's nakedness and near fall, she snapped, "Barney stuck a note under the door; I just noticed it while I was getting dressed. He wants to talk to me before breakfast; I don't know what the fuck he wants, but I'm going. Maybe I can get him to go for a walk—it'll beat eating that crap downstairs again."

As abruptly as Gloria came, she was gone, and Lizzie was left shaking with anger.

On top of it, she now faced the distasteful task of eating another meal in Sydney Slating's company. If her stomach had not been rumbling for the last 20 minutes, she would have skipped the meal herself, but she was ravenous.

'God, why did I think this was the right thing to do?' she thought miserably.

> <

Still stretching, Barn followed Arnie down the stairs.

The breakfast hour was nearly at hand.

Sydney Slating was nowhere in sight, but Lizzie Tidman and Jane Slating were already in their seats sharing some mindless banter. Behind the lengthy table, George Parker, looking grim, poured coffee.

"So, where's your friend this morning?" Jane asked the other woman, ignoring the man who placed a cup of coffee in front of her. She did not bother to say 'thanks', because she knew it would be a waste of breath; it was a safe bet that her host would not say 'you're welcome'.

"She's gone..." Lizzie began, but looked up quickly when it registered on her that she was hearing two sets of footsteps on the staircase.

Sydney Slating had already gone out, she had seen him with her own eyes, and Gloria said she was going downstairs to meet Barney at least an hour ago—only one person should be coming downstairs.

She stared in frank amazement at the two young men who had reached the bottom of the stairs, and were walking toward the table.

"What's wrong?" Jane Slating asked, seeing the younger woman's puzzled expression.

Ignoring the Texan's question, Lizzie asked, "Barn, where's Glo?"

"I have no idea. Why?" Barn replied, as he and Arnie settled into the same seats they had taken the previous morning.

"Hi, Jane," he said to the other woman seated at the long table. "Where's your brother this morning?"

"He left for his walk a bit later this morning; he's going to skip breakfast, I think."

Looking ashamed for something she had played no part in, she said, "Breakfast didn't go too well yesterday."

"Not your fault," Barn said easily, before looking toward Lizzie again, and asking, "Why'd you ask me about Gloria? I haven't seen her since I left the tavern last night."

With her puzzled look changing to fear, Lizzie asked, "Didn't you leave a note asking Glo to meet you before breakfast?"

Barn glanced at Arnie; bells were sounding, but neither one could quite distinguish the tune yet.

"No I didn't. We just came out of our room for the first time now," he answered. "What are you talking about?"

Her eyes locking onto Barn's as she grew steadily paler, the receptionist from Maryland responded, "When I was taking a shower, Glo barged in, and said she'd just noticed a note you'd stuck under the door. She said you wanted to talk to her before breakfast…she was gonna ask you to go for a walk afterwards."

Tactfully omitting the rest of what Gloria said, Lizzie concluded, "I figured you'd gone."

Barn shook his head slowly from side to side. "I didn't write a note, Lizzie," he said again.

In a gentle tone, because he could feel the fear emanating from the young woman seated at the head of the table, he asked, "Do you have it…the note, I mean?"

Lizzie, born with the habit of sticking things into her pockets, stood up, and dug into her jeans. Pulling out a folded scrap of paper, she held it out, explaining, "Here, I picked it up from the foot of Glo's bed. I don't know why, really…" Her voice trailed away as she held the note out to Barn.

Taking the clumsily torn out notebook page from Lizzie's slender fingers, Barn read aloud: "Glo—I need to talk to you. Meet me outside at 8—Barney."

He looked up, shaking his head, and said, "I didn't write this." Holding the note out for Arnie's inspection, he added, "That's not my handwriting."

Arnie took the paper from his friend, and quickly studied the words scribbled on it.

Looking up at the others, he said, "It's signed 'Barney'... Barn never uses that name. He'll answer to it, his parents call him that, and sometimes I do, but he'd never..."

A disturbing thought hit him, and he stopped speaking. He remembered calling his partner 'Barney' at breakfast yesterday morning. Unintentionally, he had led everyone present to conclude that Barn was called 'Barney'.

Looking silently from face to face, Arnie wondered which one belonged to the note's author...and he wondered where Sydney Slating had actually gone.

Chapter 12

Brushing dust off of his jeans and stomping it off of his boots, Russell Johnson, Maple Grove Junction's resident state trooper, banged on the peeling doors of the Honeybees 'n Raspberries Inn.

Tall and broad-shouldered, the sandy-haired Johnson was 47 years old. A good man and a hardworking one, Russ put in more hours as a carpenter than he did as a law officer. His late wife, Phyllis, whom he had lost to cancer two years earlier, used to call him the law-enforcing door re-enforcer.

That description still fit; even this morning when his cell phone came to life with the call from his rat-faced uncle by marriage, he was across the green replacing the broken door on the Grissom's tool shed.

The battered door had been in sorry shape for at least a year, but Whit was a great one for putting things off.

Gretchen finally called Russ herself yesterday morning, and told him she thought she had heard an animal in the shed the night before.

'Probably those damned raccoons' Russ had thought at the time, and understood that the old woman wanted the door replaced before the masked squatters moved in.

George's call was an interesting one.

The Grove was a dull place. During his tenure as the resident state trooper, the only calls Russ had taken about disappearances had involved tools and the occasional pig, but he felt up to the task at hand.

Wordlessly, the innkeeper opened the door to the trooper, who stepped inside, immediately saying, "You said something about a missing person on the phone a minute ago, George. What's this all about?"

His host, who thought the best thing about being a mechanic was that car innards did not expect him to carry on conversations, stepped aside to let him pass.

The reluctant innkeeper did not invite his late wife's nephew to sit down, but Russ sat anyway. Pulling a chair out from the long table, he settled sideways on it after placing his notebook on the table's edge and digging a Bic out of his shirt pocket.

Clad in beat up old jeans and a red plaid work shirt, the trooper stretched his long legs out into the room, showing off his well-worn boots to their fullest advantage.

With his arms casually crossed over his chest, he appeared completely at ease, but his lively brown eyes were alert.

"Girl's gone missing from here," George Parker answered, his lack of concern evident in his voice.

As far as Parker was concerned, a guest leaving the inn before breakfast was a good thing. There would be one less person waiting for an opportunity to strike up a conversation with him about the leaves or some other trivial nonsense.

He did feel some emotion this morning, though—no one ate breakfast, so he had wasted both time and money.

"What's her name?" Russ asked, taking up notebook and pen.

"Gloria Baines," Parker answered.

"Can you tell me exactly what happened?" Russ asked, doubting that the man before him, whose normal expression made him look as though he sucked limes, would actually be able to help.

Parker did not disappoint him.

"All I know" he began, "is her friend claimed another guest, some fairy kid, left a note for this Gloria girl to meet him before breakfast. The fairy says it's not his handwriting, and his friend says his name's not 'Barney' it's 'Barn'."

"Stupidest mess I've ever seen; you figure it out," the disagreeable innkeeper said with a scowl. "I gotta get back to the kitchen, and throw away food nobody ate."

As Parker slunk back toward his kitchen, Johnson rolled his eyes; nothing George Parker ever said made much sense, but this time he even had himself beat.

A woman was missing, and he was worrying about wasted food—the man could serve as Captain on the ship of fools!

Russ let the gay slur pass for now; Parker was an idiot. He wrote down what the man said, and rested his notebook on his muscular, denim-covered thigh.

Turning all the way around in his chair, so that he was looking toward the doorway George Parker had vanished through, he called out, "George, where are your other guests now?" He stuck the Bic behind his right ear, as he looked toward the kitchen.

George shouted back, "After I talked to you, I told 'em you were fixing Grissom's shed, 'cuz that old battle axe said a raccoon or somethin' was in it the other night, but you'd be here when you were done. The blond girl started gettin' hysterical—she was driving me 'round the bend with it.

I told 'em all to go up to their rooms; I didn't want 'em down here fussing at me anymore."

Disregarding his host's callous remarks for the same reason he had let the earlier slur pass, Russ said, "Have the folks come down one at a time, would ya'?"

Grumbling under his breath, George emerged from the kitchen, and headed for the stairs.

'What a jackass' Russ thought, craning his neck to watch the older man mount the steps. Like many other people who had known, or been related to, the sweet, loving Bessie Parker, Russ Johnson wondered what she had seen in the heartless, mean-spirited mechanic who was climbing to the second floor.

Since the day she died, Russ felt that his aunt's heart attack had been a long time in coming; it was a miracle George Parker had not brought one on sooner. He had nearly turned spousal abuse into a religion.

> <

Before any of the guests had a chance to come downstairs, Sydney Slating returned.

He looked at Russ Johnson, still seated casually at the table, and, obviously thinking the trooper was a lazy employee, growled at him, "Y'all need to haul the garbage away…or are you waiting for all the flies out back to do it for you?"

"I don't know what George is training his flies to do," Russ answered.

While he disliked his unexpected visitor straight away, he was glad to have something he could come down on Parker for; he had never been able to nail him for anything else, but failure to haul garbage away in a timely fashion presented a legitimate health concern. "I'll talk to him about it, though, Mister...?"

"Slating...Sydney Slating."

"I'll speak to him about that, Mr. Slating...you can bet I will," Russ assured the sinewy man standing before him.

Taking his notebook from his knee and retrieving the Bic from its perch behind his ear, he made a brief entry.

With a mind toward subtle interrogation, he said nonchalantly, "I came straight across the green myself, so I didn't see the backyard. You didn't come outta the woods back there, did ya'? Those paths are pretty well overgrown. If you got tripped up in all the vines back there, you could really get yourself hurt."

Slating shook his head, "No...I walked about three miles down the road, and then came back the same way. I didn't know there were any trails up into the woods."

He was beginning to look puzzled now; if the man in the chair was not an employee of the inn's, who was he?

"What's going on?" he asked.

Still not bothering to stand up, Russ motioned his guest into a chair. "Take a load off," he said. "I'm the resident state trooper, Russ Johnson. George called me this morning, and said a young woman's missing."

Even as he spoke the words, Russ could not help thinking that his big city counterparts would not even have answered the call until tomorrow at this time—the girl might really have gone for a walk.

'Oh well' he thought, 'nothing much else to do today anyway…Grissom's shed door's all set.'

Sydney replied, "Which girl?"

"Gloria Baines," Russ answered, studying the other man's face. He thought he seemed a bit apprehensive; his next question reflected his thought. "Friend of yours?"

"No friend of mine. I'm traveling with my sister, not some little trollop, if that's what you're aiming at," Sydney said in a voice that was cold and defensive.

"I'm not 'aiming at' anything, Mr. Slating," Russ answered. "I'm trying to work out who's who in this place…and figure out who's with whom at the same time."

His voice was calm; it took a lot to ruffle Russ Johnson's feathers. "I'll ask the question again. Did you know her?"

This time Sydney's answer was made in an entirely different tone of voice. He said, "I don't know her personally, but she's been here since Thursday, according to what she said at breakfast yesterday morning. She's traveling with another woman."

Defensive seconds earlier, Slating was the aggressor now, adding in an accusatory tone, "Yesterday was the first time they made it to the table...they were probably hung over until now."

"Did they show signs of intoxication?" Russ asked, looking up from beneath blond brows.

"No" Sydney answered, smiling unpleasantly. "They must've slept it off." With no basis for the comment at all, he added, "God knows what else they slept off...drugs maybe."

Taking another swipe at the missing woman's character, he added, "Gloria didn't show any signs of morals, either... she was flirting like the devil with one of the young fellas staying here—Barney something."

He snorted, "Turns out he's up here to marry the fella he's traveling with. It took the wind out of her sails, I'll tell ya' that. I almost laughed...ended up choking on my toast."

Despite the maliciousness of his words, Sydney looked pleased for having delivered them.

Russ Johnson thought the man sitting in front of him could hang himself without rope; he wondered if there was any chance he was related to George Parker. He was certainly mean-spirited enough.

Reducing the other man's snide remarks to the level of idle gossip, and at the same time steering the interview back in the direction he wanted it to go, Russ said, "We got to chatting right away, and I neglected to ask—can you give me your full name, occupation, address, date of birth and Social Security number?"

After scribbling Sydney's answers to the routine questions down in his notebook, Russ continued, "George Parker mentioned that someone left a note under the missing girl's door this morning. Did you hear anyone in the hallway… see anything unusual?"

Sydney Slating shook his head, and answered, "No. I left here about eight o'clock or thereabouts…"

So casually the attorney did not even realize he was being asked if someone could confirm his whereabouts, Russ said, "I enjoy a walk in the mornings, too…gotta be alone, right?"

"Yes," Slating answered. "I always walk alone in the morning; it clears my head for the day."

"Same here," Russ said.

With a nod and a smile apparently intended to show that he was happy to cooperate with the law, Sydney added, "I don't know what time you're talking about, but I didn't hear anything unusual, or see anyone in the hallway, before I left here."

Russ closed his notebook. "Thanks," he said.

Chapter 13

The next party to join Russ Johnson at the table on the morning of Gloria's disappearance was Jane Slating.

Immaculately dressed in hunter green slacks and a coral pink sweater, the legal assistant entered the room just as her brother was standing up to leave.

"Sydney, what took you so long? Did you see Gloria anywhere?" she asked.

Her voice was openly concerned; her brother had told her he was going to miss breakfast this morning because he knew he had made a fool of himself the day before, and she had believed him—now, she was not sure she did.

"I just got back; I didn't see her or anyone else...."

"But she's missing, Sydney," Jane cut in. "Are you sure you didn't see her, Syd…maybe on your way out? Everyone's terribly worried…"

Jane's impromptu interrogation would have continued, but her brother cut her off with a waspish, "I'm going up to take a shower now."

He gave Russ a short nod, brushed by his sister, and headed up the stairs.

'Charming bastard' Russ thought, asking his new visitor to take a seat.

As soon as they got the perfunctory questions out of the way, he queried, "Mr. Slating is your brother?"

Unnerved by the disappearance of Gloria Baines and worried about her brother, Jane was already fidgeting with imaginary lint on her sweater as she answered, "Yes… older by 11 months, officer."

"It's trooper, but just call me Russ."

"I imagine I was a bit of a surprise to my parents…Russ," she smiled. "I doubt they planned to have two children born in the same year." Another invisible particle of fuzz was removed from the nicely fitting sweater.

Russ smiled back at the woman; in good cop/bad cop, Russ Johnson would always be the good one. He would find out why the woman seated before him seemed suspicious of her brother, but he would take the scenic route.

"Your brother said the missing woman was flirting like the devil yesterday morning with a young man staying here. Did you have that impression as well?"

Jane cringed. "What has Sydney been saying?"

Then, before Russ could answer, she stated forthrightly, "My brother's just gone through a very bitter divorce, and I'm afraid he's feeling rather down on women these days—especially redheads, like his ex-wife."

"Is your brother a violent man?" Russ asked, his voice as direct as Jane's had been.

"No" she answered, shaking her head. "In fact, he's very squeamish, actually; he's terrified of bugs." She folded her hands in her lap, not seeming to know what else to do with them.

Her gaze was steadier than her hands, and she looked directly into the trooper's eyes. She knew she had to tell him this even though it might cast suspicion on Sydney.

"Before my brother left this morning he told me that he was going out, and wouldn't be back for breakfast. He made an ass of himself at yesterday's morning meal, and I thought he might have had the decency to realize that himself...he used to be such a gentlemen once."

Russ flipped a few pages of his notebook back, and scratched out the 'check for health hazard' comment he had jotted down earlier. If the man had a fear of bugs, there only needed to be two or three of them flying around together to set him off.

He continued his line of questioning, by asking, "So, was there a lot of flirting going on?"

Jane replied, "Gloria was smiling and making puppy eyes at one of the young men staying here, Barney Moss. It was harmless—just the silly things young girls do to catch a fella's eye…you know, giggling and batting their lashes."

The woman seated in the chair recently vacated by Sydney Slating shrugged her own shoulders, as though the art of flirting was foreign and just a bit silly to her.

Watching her, Russ thought the slight shoulder action in and of itself was very attractive, and wondered how such a naturally charming woman could be unaware of her own ability to catch a man's eye.

He thought the men in Texas must be blind, and thanked God for his own 20/20 vision as he answered noncommittally, "It's been a few years since anyone tried to catch my eye, but I know it when I see it. Go ahead."

Jane smiled at him; she liked what she saw too, and felt more than a little bit foolish. The man was questioning her, and she was starting to feel like a giddy schoolgirl.

She cleared her throat, and tried to put on her business face. "As I said, she fancied the boy. Between you and I, that's exactly what he looks like—a boy. He's quite a good-looking one...little as a minute, though."

"How old would you say Gloria is?" the trooper asked, suddenly finding himself smiling foolishly. "School age, or grown?"

Jane's silvery laugh floated above the table as she answered, "She didn't really say, at least not that I recall, but she's young; I wouldn't think she's more than 25."

Russ made a few notes. "Go ahead, Jane. You were telling me about the flirting." The voice of his conscience chimed in, 'You were flirting with her, and she knows it...now you feel like a jackass, and you should'.

"Well, what started it" Jane began, "was that I'd asked Gloria what brought her and her friend..."

"Who's her friend, Jane? No one's said the name to me yet," Russ briefly interrupted.

"Her name's Lizzie Tidman," Jane answered. "She seems like a nice girl. She'll be down to talk to you later, but right now the poor little thing's upstairs crying her heart out. I tried to comfort her a bit, but she's scared to death."

The trooper nodded his sandy blond head sympathetically, and then asked, "What did bring the girls to Vermont?"

Jane answered, "They gave the usual reasons all tourists give, I suppose. They said they wanted to see the leaves, do some shopping and have a bit of fun."

Chuckling, Jane added, "This was funny, they thought they might meet some cute guys."

The trooper smiled, commenting, "I've never noticed any cute guys, but then again, I've never looked for any. Cute women are more my speed."

He was thinking of sticking his pen in his eye—anything to get himself focused again; he could not believe the words that had just come out of his mouth. His conscience cautioned him, 'Stop acting like a hot-to-trot teenager, Russ."

"What happened next?" he asked.

Jane responded, "I don't think I'd say 'next' necessarily, because this happened at the same time. When Gloria said they'd hoped to meet a cute guy or two, she looked directly over at Barney Moss…"

Suddenly feeling she should explain something that she knew would be coming up in a little while, she interrupted the flow of her story to say, "All through breakfast yesterday morning, his friend called him Barney. This morning, after he read the note, and it was signed 'Barney' his friend said that's not the name he uses…"

"George Parker said something about that," Russ interrupted briefly. "Can you explain it a bit? George wasn't as clear as he could have been."

"Yes, certainly," Jane answered politely. "From what was said this morning, I gather that his parents call him by the diminutive form of his name, and sometimes his friend does too...but he's a grown man, after all, not a little boy...so, even though he'll answer to 'Barney' he would never sign it—he'd sign 'Barn'."

Russ nodded; Jane's concise explanation was far better than Parker's had been. Force of habit was a powerful thing; a man accustomed to signing his name a particular way was not likely to change it on a quickly scrawled note.

"Anyway" the legal assistant said picking up her story again, "my point was that she looked directly at him, and said something about the only men they'd met so far were older than the hills, and married for a thousand years."

Jane Slating smiled, and shrugged her slender shoulders again, at the same time giving Russ Johnson another reason to gouge out one of his eyes.

"Was that the end of it?" he asked, thinking it could not possibly be. To his ears, it did not sound like the missing Gloria had been flirting like the devil with anyone.

It also sounded like Jane understood the significance of the 'Barney' vs. 'Barn' signature; both George Parker and

Sydney Slating appeared ignorant of it...of course, that could just have been a normal condition.

"For the flirting it was," Jane answered. "When Gloria asked him what he and his friend, Arnie Kotkin...if I didn't say the name before, and I don't think I did..."

"Barney and Arnie?" the trooper interrupted. He had to chuckle. "They must be teased as much as a couple whose names are Jack and Jill. Small wonder he prefers to be called 'Barn'."

Laughing suddenly, Jane said, "Isn't that cute? Until this minute, I didn't catch it."

She shook her head, still smiling, as she said, "What I was about to say, though, was that Gloria asked what the two boys were doing in Vermont, and Barney...Barn...said they were getting married on Wednesday."

With a sympathetic smile for the missing young woman's discomfort, Jane said, "The poor girl looked so embarrassed, and my brother behaved like a fool...he actually started to laugh at her, and ended up choking on his toast."

"Did the men say anything...I mean, did they seem angry because of her question?" Russ asked.

"No. I think they may have felt a little bit embarrassed for her, but they didn't seem upset otherwise. In fact, the four of them spent the day together."

"Did they?"

"Yes. Sydney had gone upstairs…we went out ourselves later, but I suppose he was in our bathroom just then. Anyway, I was sitting just here, right in this chair, actually, when I looked out the window. The boys and Gloria were talking by their car, and after just a minute they all climbed in. It looked like Gloria yelled something to Lizzie then, and she walked over and got into the car too. They drove off, and were gone all day."

"Did you happen to notice what time they got home?"

"They came in at different times, actually," Jane said.

"Sydney and I had gone out for an early supper, and he went right upstairs when we got home. I was sitting here at the table looking at the paper when Barn came in. I'd just looked at my watch a minute or so earlier, so I can tell you that it was shortly before eight o'clock. I asked him if he was alone, which was stupid, because, obviously, he was, and he answered that his friend and Lizzie had gone to the movies, and Gloria was still over at the tavern."

"Did you see anyone else come in?" Russ prodded.

Jane nodded, and answered, "I saw Gloria come in at about ten o'clock. She headed straight for the stairs, without saying a word; at breakfast she'd been quite talkative, so I asked her if everything was OK, and she said it was. Mr. Parker came in almost immediately after her, and stomped out to the kitchen for a little while. When he came back in here saying he wanted to watch TV, I went up to the room."

Russ' notebook and Bic were getting a workout this morning. "What about the other two?" he asked. "Did you hear them come in?"

"I'm not much of a night owl, truthfully. I'd just had my shower, and gotten into bed, when I heard Lizzie and Arnie in the hallway. The rooms upstairs are set up two toward the front of the house and two toward the back. The hallway, naturally, is between them, so I heard their conversation quite clearly."

"Can you tell me about it?" Russ asked, not bothering to mention that he was familiar with the floor plan.

"Certainly," was Jane's reply. Straightening a bit in her chair—the seats did get uncomfortable after any length of time—she said, "I heard Arnie say, 'I wonder if the two deadbeats are asleep yet', and she answered, 'Probably… see you guys in the morning'."

"Do you have any idea what time that was?"

"Probably about 11," Jane answered. "I could kick myself for not looking at my watch," she added, raising her arm slightly. "I never take it off, except in the shower, but I guess I was just too sleepy to bother."

A frown found a home on her lips briefly, as she said, "Who would have thought one night could make such a difference?"

Russ shook his head, and then answered, "I'm afraid, unless they've got something to do with it, no one could have predicted this, Jane."

He added, "Don't worry about not checking the time on your watch. Whatever happened here happened this morning, not last night. I'm just trying to get a fix on where everyone was…it's not a big deal."

"OK," Jane responded. "Is that everything?"

Russ answered, "Not quite…I just have one last question, Jane. Did you hear anyone in the hall early this morning?"

She thought about it for a minute. "Sydney left our room shortly before eight o'clock this morning. Not terribly long after that, I heard a door across the hallway closing, and right after that, I heard footsteps going down the stairs; I think now that it was probably Gloria, but I didn't hear or see anything else."

She added as an afterthought, "I didn't leave our room until at least 15 minutes later."

"Anything during the night?"

"No" Jane replied quickly, and then added, "but it is an old place…I suppose I heard the usual creaks."

"The old places do settle at night," Russ said casually, but he wrote 'Jane Slating suspects her brother'.

Chapter 14

Arnie was the next guest to visit the makeshift interrogation room, and after running through the routine questions he answered the more important ones thoughtfully, and with great detail. As a certain detective in Lawton, New York had pointed out over a year ago, Arnie Kotkin had a head for details.

"Tell me about the day yesterday…start with breakfast," the trooper directed. The young man whose routine answers had included his former occupation and current educational goals, gave an excellent accounting of the events at George Parker's breakfast table yesterday.

"When Barn and I got downstairs, everyone else was already at the table," Arnie said, beginning his story with a statement of fact.

Casting an eye toward the chair the absent redhead had occupied yesterday, he explained, "Gloria sat at that end of the table, and Lizzie Tidman was at the opposite end. Jane and Sydney Slating were sitting on the side of the table by the window...I'm pretty sure Jane was seated to Sydney's left. Barn and I sat down on this side of the table, and he was closest to Gloria...'Glo', her friend calls her."

Russ was impressed by the remembered details; in his mind's eye, he could clearly see the people gathered around the table yesterday morning.

"What was breakfast conversation like?" Russ asked. He was not sure it mattered, really, if everything happened the way Jane Slating explained it, but when one guest from an inn went missing, and the other guests were still here to talk about it, common sense told the trooper that even one detail remembered by one guest but not by others, could be crucial.

Arnie answered, "We'd all been here different lengths of time, and yesterday was the first day we'd had breakfast together. I guess we made the usual small talk strangers make...our names, why we chose Vermont for a vacation, our occupations...those kinds of things."

He smiled, "Jane Slating really was the one who kept things going. She asked both the girls what brought them up here. Gloria said they wanted to see the scenery, have some fun, take a bunch of pictures and, maybe, meet some cute guys."

Even hearing the comment the second time, Russ grinned. "Obviously, she's never been to Vermont before," he said.

Arnie Kotkin laughed, his smile lighting up his hazel eyes. "That seems to be the truth," he agreed. "From what we can see, there isn't much in the way of fun, and, apparently, Barn and I are the two youngest guys in town, but the scenery's nice, so the pictures should be worth the trip."

The trooper had to agree with the younger man's assessment of Maple Grove Junction—the place was pretty dull—but the future college professor had just said something Jane Slating had alluded to. Lizzie had also been asked why she was there, but Jane had not mentioned her answer.

"What reason did Lizzie give for being here?" he asked.

Putting a finger to his lip for a second, Arnie concentrated before answering, "I think she said her family…at least her mother…was from Vermont. I remember Jane making the comment that the trip was sort of a homecoming for Lizzie."

Thinking he would be in danger of writer's cramp by the time he finished speaking with this young man, Russ put his next question out. "I've heard that Gloria seemed to have her eye on your friend…Barnard, is it?" he asked.

"No, it's Barnaby," Arnie answered, and then explained, "He goes by Barn, unless he has to say his last name too— then he'll say Barnaby Moss, because, obviously, 'Barn Moss' sounds asinine."

The fair-haired man smiled, adding, "Either he was a really tough delivery, or his mother just wasn't thinking."

Russell Johnson grinned at the remark as much as at the name, before saying, "That brings up my next question, Arnie. I've been told that Ms. Baines found a note in her room this morning."

He paused for a second to jot down a reminder to himself, 'get the note', before continuing, "The note was signed 'Barney', but both you and he have said it was not his handwriting. That right?"

Arnie nodded, his golden curls bouncing, "Yes, that's right."

He stood up, and poked his long fingers into his back pocket. "I'm the last one who looked at it, and I just stuck it in my pocket. I almost forgot I had it."

He handed the note over to Russ, who read it in a whispered voice, "Glo—I need to talk to you. Meet me outside at 8—Barney."

Looking up into the hazel eyes of the young man still standing in front of him, Russ said, "Barn didn't write it and didn't shove it under the door. You're sure of that?"

"Yes, positive, for three reasons," Arnie answered, resuming his seat. "First off, it's not his handwriting. Barn's right-handed, but this note looks like a lefty wrote it."

He traced one long forefinger in the air, demonstrating the different slant of the letters formed by a right-handed person, as opposed to a left-handed individual.

Russ glanced at the note again quickly, and nodded his head. The writing did slant in the opposite direction; he could see that it appeared to have been written by a 'lefty' as the other man put it.

"Second, it was signed 'Barney'."

Conclusively, he stated, "Like I just said, he goes by 'Barn'. His parents call him 'Barney' a lot, and sometimes I do, but if you ask him his name, he's not gonna say 'Barney'. When I saw the note this morning, I remembered that I called him 'Barney' yesterday at breakfast. Because I said that, everyone at the table assumed that was the name he used."

Staring directly into Johnson's eyes, Arnie added, "I think someone in this house knows exactly where Gloria Baines is right now."

Even as he heard the young man's words, the trooper knew he was not tossing out a vague possibility; he was stating what looked like an undeniable fact. He nodded his head, and said, "I agree with you, but just to satisfy my curiosity, what was the third reason?" he asked.

Arnie Kotkin was both intelligent and honest; it was an engaging combination. Grinning, as color unexpectedly rose to his cheeks, he said, "The third reason is how I know he didn't shove it under the door…he was still buried under the covers. I couldn't even interest him in taking a shower with me."

Russ never gave another person's sexual orientation much thought one way or the other. If he had, he would probably have said that a monogamous same-sex couple was the same as a monogamous two-sex couple in his eyes—but he had to admit that Jane Slating's earlier mention of taking a shower had presented a much more enjoyable mental image.

Getting back to the point of his questioning, he said, "Just a couple more points about this morning…did you hear anyone outside the girls' door?"

"No…but I had gone in for my shower around 7:30 this morning, and if Gloria thought she was meeting Barn downstairs at eight o'clock, she would probably have been leaving just around the time I was getting out of the shower…the water may still have been running."

Russ inclined his head slightly, saying, "That's highly possible." With his next breath he said, "What can you tell me about the rest of the day?"

Arnie grinned, "Lizzie's a nice girl…very nice; Gloria's got a moody streak in her, though."

"Really?"

Never anything but honest, Arnie continued, "Yes, really. I've never seen one person have so many mood swings in the course of a day…"

"Bipolar?" Russ offered.

"Bitchy," Arnie countered. "Let me backtrack for a second" he said, as a prelude to his version of the flirtation incident.

"She was giving Barn the eye at breakfast," he began. "You know the drill—giggling, batting her eyes, smiling at him. I noticed that he looked a little bit uncomfortable, and when she asked what our plans were for the day, he was only too eager to tell her we were going for a marriage license."

He grinned suddenly, remembering the look on Barn's face as he realized he was being hit on, and continued, "I think if he'd said 'nothing particular', or something equally vague, she would've suggested getting together, but he told her we were going for a marriage license. She did have the good grace to look embarrassed, and I think we both felt kind of bad for her that way…but not Sydney Slating. He started to laugh, and ended up choking on his toast."

Russ wrote, 'S.S. is a bastard' in his notebook.

"Go ahead," he prompted. "What was the rest of the day like?" He still did not know how important any of this was, but Kotkin's details were good, and he thought if there were anything here, he would find it if he listened long enough.

"After breakfast, we were in the parking lot, and she came running up to us, telling us she was sorry for putting Barn on the spot that way," Arnie explained. "Then, without missing a beat, she proceeded to invite herself and Lizzie along with us! She told us we could do our stuff first, and then we could drive them to some antiques shops…like it was a great honor for us, or something."

The blond narrator admitted, "I really could've put an end to it there, but I acted kind of like my father, who's pretty henpecked, to be truthful, and put it to Barn. He's got a little bit of a temper, and he rammed it back at me. He told her they could come along, just to bust my balls."

The trooper scribbled, smiling appreciatively at the same time. "My late wife used to do that stuff to me, too," he said, with no conscious thought of how the words sounded.

Arnie burst out laughing at the unexpected comment. "He's not actually my wife," he chuckled.

"I'm sorry," Russ said, beginning to smile uncomfortably, despite the sincere words of apology. "I didn't mean it to sound that way…no offense meant."

The other man shook his golden curls. "That's all right," he said. "We all stick our feet into our mouths from time to time…Barn's a pro at it lately…don't worry about it. No offense was taken."

"OK, then" Russ began, "to get back to the outing yesterday, Barn let them come along because you didn't put your foot down and say they couldn't?"

"Yes, that's right," Arnie grinned. Tying up the loose strands of the trooper's embarrassment, he added, "Typical wife."

Growing serious then, he explained, "We were both pissed about Gloria inviting them along, and we were equally annoyed with each other. We settled down, though, and didn't have too bad a time, Gloria's mood swings aside."

He shook his head again and quipped, "I'm glad Barn doesn't suffer from PMS—he can be bad enough without it."

Russ flashed a quick smile, and then asked, "What time did you get back?"

"I guess it was around 6:30. Gretchen Grissom waved to us, and after Barn parked the car, we walked back over there for a sandwich. Out of the blue, Lizzie decided she wanted to go to the movies, so the two of us ended up doing that after we ate…we left before eight o'clock."

Arnie swallowed, and then concluded, "Barn said he was gonna have another beer, and then go back to take a shower; Gloria thought another beer sounded good, or maybe a couple, and so she was just planning to hang around the tavern for awhile."

A faraway look clouding his eyes, he said, "That's the last time I saw her."

> <

Lizzie Tidman finished relaying her personal information to Russ Johnson, and gave a synopsis of the breakfast scene that was close to both Jane and Arnie's—not quite as specific, but obviously they all remembered the same things, just through different eyes.

"We had a pretty good day," Lizzie explained, in response to an inquiry about the antiquing trip.

"After breakfast, Gloria and I were on our way out, when she saw the guys near their car. She ran over to apologize… neither of them acted, you know, girly, at breakfast, and we didn't realize they were gay."

Having just met Arnie Kotkin, Russ knew exactly what she meant. He did not act 'girly' at all.

"They're nice guys" Lizzie said, "and neither of 'em got mad about it." In a softer voice, she added, "I think they must've both gotten pretty mad after Glo invited us along, though."

"What makes you say that?" Russ asked.

"Well" the slender blond began, "I didn't actually hear her inviting us along, because I was still back by the inn, but she yelled to me to come over there. She said she'd told the guys we'd ride with them…not they'd asked us to… she TOLD them we would."

Tucking a stray lock of hair behind her right ear, Lizzie added, "She's, like, authoritative."

"You mean she's pushy?" Russ prodded, one eyebrow raised inquisitively.

"Yeah…sometimes," Lizzie admitted.

The trooper sat back in his chair, and studied the young woman's face. He could not decide if she was embarrassed by Gloria's behavior, angered by it, or simply worried.

"What makes you say both of the men were mad, Lizzie? Did they say something to you?" Russ asked.

"No, they were OK to me" Lizzie answered, "but I could tell they were mad about something, and I had to assume it was Glo inviting us along, because they'd been fine with each other at breakfast."

Shifting in her seat, a movement that had become a routine performance for visitors to that wretched piece of furniture, she related what, obviously, had been the aftermath of the incident Arnie Kotkin had related.

"I could, like, feel the tension between them when I first got in the car," Lizzie explained. "Like I said, they were OK to me, but they acted kind of impatient with each other, and with Glo…not that she'd notice—or care."

Russ jotted, 'G.B. sounds like a piece of work' on his notebook, and then moved on. "Tell me about the rest of the day."

"OK," she said. "We went on their errands with them, and waited in the car while they got their marriage license. After that, the four of us went off to some antiques places. On the way back, we stopped for lunch at this little place called 'Sandwiches'…that's all they had, too…"

"I know the place," Russ commented. "What time did you get back?"

"About 6:30" Lizzie answered, and then elaborated, "When we got here, the tavern lady was outside, and she waved to us, and said to come over, so we decided to leave my stuff, which was just some curtains, in their car."

She interrupted herself with the unexpected exclamation, "Shit! I never got 'em out of the car." Quickly getting back on track, she said, "Anyway, we went over to the tavern for another sandwich and a beer."

"How long did you stay at the tavern?" Russ asked.

"For Arnie and I, it wasn't terribly long…a little over an hour I guess. We left for the 8:15 movie. We talked about it first, and asked the tavern lady, Gretchen, where the place was. She told us how to get there, what she thought was playing, and said the popcorn was good. I wanted to go, and so did Arnie, but Glo and Barn didn't want to, so we left 'em here."

"That the last time you talked to your friend?" Russ asked.

"Kind of…the last time I talked to her was in the tavern—she was asleep when I got back just around eleven o'clock. She talked to me this morning when I was in the shower; she stuck her head in, and told me she'd just found a note from Barney…did you see it?"

"Yes, I have it. Go on."

An annoyed look crossing her face, Lizzie explained, "She yanked the shower door back so hard, I nearly jumped out of my skin…I nearly fell…but she never apologized for scaring me. She just barged in, and then stomped out."

Russ thought the absent Gloria sounded every bit as charming as Arnie had described her.

Chapter 15

Russ Johnson finally made the acquaintance of Barnaby Moss.

Watching the young man descend the stairs, he wondered what the missing woman had seen. As Jane Slating had said earlier, he was good looking; he was also the tiniest grown man Russ had ever set his eyes on.

To the trooper's mind, someone who looked to be about 12 would not have been 'flirting like the devil with' material, unless the girl doing the flirting was 10 years old.

Russ had the immediate impression that the young man walking toward the table could not strangle, stab or bludgeon anyone without first climbing on a chair to reach their neck or vital organs; if the missing girl turned out to be the murdered girl, he thought Moss was in the clear— unless she had died from a bullet wound.

Barn took the hot seat, and looked into the trooper's dark eyes...they were not as dark as his own, but they were close.

"Hi," he said. He was the first person to utter the greeting.

"Hi," the trooper answered. As with his previous visitors, Russ got the routine questions out of the way first.

In response to Barn's last answer, his age, he said, "You don't look 25."

Barn replied easily, "Actually, I'll be 26 next month, that's probably why." He smiled, revealing perfect white teeth. He had dimples when he grinned, and they succeeded in making him look even younger than he already appeared; the jeans and Springstein T-shirt he was wearing did not add years to his age.

"I think we need to start with breakfast yesterday, which seems to be when all of the guests here met for the first time," Russ explained to his new witness. "What can you tell me about breakfast yesterday...what was the conversation like?"

Barn began to speak, telling essentially the same story that the others had told; his details were as clear as his partner's had been. He described the seating arrangement, the meager bill of fare and the unusual turn the topic of conversation had taken vis-à-vis the girls not having been seen at breakfast until that morning.

"Let's move on to the rest of the day, then," Russ Johnson said. There was no reason, at least none that was immediately evident, for Russ to assume that the guests had quietly gathered upstairs and rehearsed their collective story; therefore, he concluded that Monday morning's repast had gone exactly the way it had been described to him.

"OK," Barn answered. "Anything particular, or do I just start at the top?"

"Start with the parking lot," Russ responded. "Another guest mentioned seeing Gloria talking to you and your friend in the parking lot after breakfast; you all left in the same car. Tell me about that."

As with breakfast, Russ was prepared to hear another version of the same story—the only difference being the personal perspective of the speaker.

"I suppose everyone's told you Arnie and I are up here this week to get married…tomorrow, in fact," Barn said. With a broad grin, he added, "Even if no one else did, I hope Arnie mentioned it."

When the trooper inclined his head, Barn continued, "We had to go for the license yesterday morning, and the girls tagged along. It was Gloria's idea, but I said I didn't mind, primarily because Arnie wasn't man enough to say he did. The girls had a few words to start with and Lizzie got a little ruffled, but they worked it out…"

"How's that?" Russ asked. This was the first time he had heard that there was a quarrel between the two young women.

"Umm, nothing major," Barn said. "I think she was just embarrassed that Gloria asked if they could go with us; then Gloria made it worse by making a bad joke about how stupid Lizzie had been the day before, driving right by a shop she wanted to stop in…just little catty stuff, really," the diminutive man observed. "Not that Arnie and I weren't being completely childish in the front seat, because we were…"

"Because you had said they could come along, when Arnie didn't tell them 'no' in the first place?"

Barn laughed, and admitted, "Caught making a catty remark of my own. It's true, though. Arnie didn't want 'em along, and I certainly didn't, but he gave me this stupid look over the top of the car, like 'get us out of this', and I got ticked off. I figured I'd say they could come, and maybe the next time something like that came up, he'd learn to say 'no' straight off."

Russ remembered words he had spoken not long ago— words that had sounded all right in his brain, yet ridiculous when they hit his eardrums, but they still applied.

The accounting both men had given sounded for all the world like an ordinary spat between any couple.

He glanced at his watch. It had been a long day, and it was barely noon. Tapping the end of his pen on his notebook, he said, "OK…so, how did the trip with the girls work out?"

Barn brushed a few locks of dark hair away from his forehead, as he continued, "Well, after we left the town hall, we drove the girls to the shops they wanted to go to…"

Knowing what was available in the tourist-trap shops, Russ interrupted with a grin, "Anyone buy anything?"

"Not much…Lizzie picked up some old curtains, which are still in my car, come to think of it," Barn answered. "The only other thing any of us bought was lunch. We stopped in Falling Rock Junction…"

Smiling again, Russ asked, "How was it at 'Sandwiches' yesterday? Did they have the baloney or the Pickle & Pimento loaf?"

Barn wrinkled his nose at the second selection, and said, "The baloney, thank God…everything from IGA, right down to the plates and napkins."

Again, Russ Johnson was impressed. He would have sworn that city people did not pay much attention to details—how could they, when their lives moved at such a quick pace?

It would scarcely be another 24 hours before the trooper realized that, not only did the young men notice everything, they were quick to make the details fit a sensible scenario.

Barn continued his story. "After we ate…and you already know it didn't take long…we thought we might just as well head back…"

"Remember what time?"

The young witness cocked his head to one side. "Not terribly late," he said. "Maybe four o'clock or so, I really didn't look at my watch."

"You didn't come straight back?" Russ asked, knowing they had to have made a few stops; it did not take over two hours to drive back from 'Sandwiches'.

Understanding that an accounting for the time was being asked for, Barn answered, "No…if we'd driven continuously for two hours, we'd have ended up in another state. The girls had their cameras with them, and we stopped dozens of times so they could take pictures—first of whatever tree they thought was good, and then pictures of each of us with the lucky tree…some pictures of the roads. It was exciting stuff."

With a grin, he added, "I'm glad the time hasn't changed yet, or a lot of those shots would have been taken in the dark."

"What time did you get back?" Russ asked, knowing the answer.

"We didn't end up getting back here until almost 6:30, I think, and by that time, we were all thirsty," Barn said. "Gretchen Grissom was outside the tavern, and she waved to us, so we parked my car and walked back. As we got up closer to the tavern, Gretchen yelled out that her husband…"

Barn interrupted himself, grinning, "Actually, she called him the old bastard, but I gather that's a pet name for him or something."

Russ Johnson allowed himself a laugh, before saying, "Yup, she calls him that all the time."

Resuming his account of the events, Barn said, "She called out that Whit and his cronies hadn't gotten into the roast beef yet, so we should come in and get some."

"What time did you leave the tavern?" Russ repeated the question he had asked two of his other visitors that morning. He got the same answer…plus a bit more.

"I left not too long after Arnie and Lizzie did, actually," Barn said, gazing out the window for a minute. He had just caught a glimpse of a dark blue Lexus passing the window; Arnie's aunt and uncle, a/k/a his parents, were here.

Giving his full attention to the trooper again, he said, "Gloria was planning on staying at the tavern for a little longer." Almost as an afterthought, he added, "I remember thinking that the old lady, Gretchen, would probably be just as happy not having Gloria come back here while her roommate was still out."

Russ Johnson looked up; it was an interesting observation, and one he had not previously heard. "What makes you say that?" he asked, already suspecting that Gretchen had made young Mr. Moss privy to her thoughts about George Parker.

Barn replied, "On Sunday night, the first time Arnie and I went into the tavern, Gretchen mentioned both of the girls, and then she told us she worries when Parker has women over here alone. She doesn't think too much of him. She said he beat his wife. I don't know if that's true or not…"

"It is," Johnson said flatly.

"OK…but, what I was gonna say was, it seems to be enough that Gretchen believes he did. She asked Arnie and I to let her know if we saw him trying to pull anything funny."

Russ nodded his sandy head, and said, "That's Gretchen all right, always thinking of other people."

Switching from the role of interrogator to the role of witness for just a minute, he explained, "Bessie Parker, George's late wife, was my aunt. She and Gretchen were best friends; if anyone else on this earth knows how mean a man George Parker is, it's Gretchen. I'd reckon Bessie confided a lot of things to her over the years. She does worry about women alone there, and she keeps me posted on what he's up to."

As he spoke, Russ Johnson studied the young man seated before him. Christ, he was tiny; he wondered exactly how much help Gretchen thought he would be. She would have had a better chance of knocking George Parker cold herself.

"Go ahead," he said, becoming the interrogator again, "What time did the others leave the tavern? I realize that you don't know when Gloria left."

"Arnie and Lizzie left just before me, like I said. They were gonna go to the movies. Gretchen told 'em the starting times were 8:15 and 10:45, I think. They left in time for the 8:15 show—probably about quarter to eight, I guess. As soon as I finished my beer, I walked back to the inn. I guess I was halfway up the stairs when I remembered Lizzie's stuff out in my car, but I was too damned lazy to go back for it…"

The interview was interrupted then by the sound of the front door opening. Helene and Jack Fentnor had arrived.

Barn quickly crossed the room to greet them, whispering urgently, "There's been some trouble here this morning. Gloria Baines, one of the other guests, is missing." He related the rest of the story, and, as he spoke, Jack's handsome face grew increasingly troubled.

When Barn finished speaking to his soon-to-be in-laws, he introduced them to Russ Johnson as Arnie's aunt and uncle.

Jack shook the trooper's hand, and then prompted, "I think you should take a look out back, trooper. Lenie and I noticed a lot of flies back there when we parked our car. We thought a garbage can might have gotten dumped over..."

This was the second mention of the flies, but the first time the possible significance had not struck him; he did not need to be told a third time.

With his notebook and pen still in hand, the trooper was making tracks for the door even before Jack finished speaking; Barn was on his heels.

Bursting out into the sunlight, the two men sprinted around the side of the house, and made for the trees behind it...and the wall of flies.

Although no one had found her until then, other than the entire fly population of Vermont, Gloria Baines was under a tree behind the inn; at least her body was...her head was in the grass about six feet away.

Chapter 16

Russ Johnson had seen some nasty accidents in his life, both of the highway and hunting ground variety—this was worse, because it was no accident.

He walked up to where the body's head should have been, and bent down for a minute to study the macabre sight; his gag reflex was hard at work, and he needed to swallow several times—as much as the grisly scene before him, the swarm of flies was making him nauseas.

Finally standing and raising his notebook, he quickly scrawled, '1 clean swing; stump looks level; no upward cut; no sign of chopping down; likely killer of approx. equal height to victim; body looks to be about 5' in length—add approx. 9" for head; victim/killer both about 5' 9" tall.'

He pocketed his notebook, and walked back to the young man who had run out of the house with him.

"OK?" the trooper asked, fully expecting that, at any moment, the young man would lose everything he had consumed in the recent past.

In an almost inaudible whisper, Barn answered, "Yeah… I'll be OK."

His ashen skin and slightly trembling frame denied the truth of his words, but he averted his eyes from the mess on the ground, and looked off toward the scarlet-hued hills beyond the inn. At the same time, he swatted at the flies waiting to join in the feeding frenzy.

Russ hated to ask the question, the answer seemed obvious, but he had to do it.

"Is that Gloria Baines?"

He watched the younger man struggling to keep it together, and half wished he would turn around and throw up; from experience gleaned on the side of a highway many years earlier, Russ knew that would be the only way for the younger man to relieve the deadly sick feeling churning around in his stomach.

To his surprise, the young man shook his head, and said even more softly, "You've already seen it, Barn; it's not going to get any worse—hold on."

Thus steeled for the sight a second time, he squared his shoulders, and took a deliberately long look at the victim's face several feet away. "That's Gloria Baines," he said, swallowing hard.

"Positive?"

"Yeah, that's her."

Johnson gave the young man a firm thump on the shoulder; Barnaby Moss was stronger than Russ would have given him credit for. The first time he had seen a dead, disfigured body himself—a highway fatality during his second week on the job—he had thrown up on his own shoes.

"I've gotta call State Police Headquarters up in Miller Junction," he told the younger man. "I've gotta say I'm glad to get this one off my hands officially, but, unofficially, I'm gonna keep my nose in it. I wanna know who the bastard was…"

He did not get to finish his thought; Jack and Helene picked that minute to come around the corner of the house.

"Is it the missing woman?" Jack called out.

"Yup…it's her," Russ answered. "Stay back, though, folks. You don't wanna see this…she's been decapitated."

"Oh my God," Helene gasped, turning toward her husband, who folded his strong arms protectively around her.

"Oh, Lord" she whispered, burying her face against Jack's broad chest, "the poor girl."

Jack hugged his wife tightly to him; there were no words he could say.

"I'll go call this in" Russ said, "and then I'll walk over to the tavern...I've got a feeling their axe is missing."

><

Her eyes scanning the interior of the shed, Gretchen saw the usual chaos—rakes, hoes, mower, hand tools, gas cans, assorted rags, baskets and spare parts were scattered around—finally, she saw the axe.

"There's my axe, Russ...right there. Nothing's missing," she said firmly.

Russ moved over to study the axe; its head looked clean, but he would have taken it anyway, just to be sure, if Whit Grissom's booming voice had not sounded from right behind him.

"Where's the big axe, Gretchen...the great big one I kept at the back?" he demanded.

"I never knew of any axe but this one, Whit" Gretchen answered, puzzled.

The old woman's expression did not go unnoticed by the state trooper, but he made no comment.

Instead, he extended one strong hand toward Whit. "Morning, Whit," he said. "Nice you could finally get outside here…girl's been killed over at 'Honeybees'. You sure you're missing a bigger axe?"

"A'ya…mine, ain't it?" the old man snapped, deliberately refusing to shake the younger man's hand; he was aptly nicknamed by his wife. He was an old bastard.

"Describe it, Whit," Russ said, pulling the notebook from his breast pocket, and taking the Bic from behind his ear. "I think it might be our murder weapon."

Gretchen's weathered face adopted a horrified expression.

Ignoring his wife's obvious distress, Whit snarled, "It looked like an axe, you jackass…a big axe, head was kinda rusty last time I used it, red handle…kept it way in the back there."

He pointed to an empty hook, and said, "It should be right there, but it ain't."

Chapter 17

Now seated at the table in the main room, Mitch Kittery, a burly, dark-haired state police sergeant, had arrived at the shabby little inn about an hour earlier.

He had already taken a preliminary look at the crime scene and the body, checked out the inn's floor plan, found out which guests were in which rooms, and was currently debriefing Russ Johnson.

Kittery jotted entries in his notebook, while Johnson read the notes he had taken just a few hours earlier.

"Here," Russ said, suddenly interrupting himself, "I got the note from Arnie Kotkin. You'll want it." He pulled the small piece of paper out from the back of his notebook, and passed it to the state police officer.

Kittery took the slightly creased note. "Was it like this when you got it from him?" he asked, running an appraising bottle-green eye over the crinkled page.

"He had it folded up in his pocket," Russ explained, crossing one long leg over the other. "He was the last one to look at it, and he'd just shoved it in his pocket…it had already been touched by several people by the time he got it…no hope for good prints, probably."

"OK" Kittery said, and laid the small piece of paper on the table. "Did you make any notes at the scene?" He was not sure what to expect; so far, Johnson seemed sharp, but Kittery had run into one or two resident state troopers around here who seemed to be little more than dog wardens.

Russ put that thought to bed early by saying, "Yes, just a couple," and then proceeding to read them aloud. He concluded by frankly admitting, "I've seen some bad accidents, but I never saw a decapitation before…hope I never do again."

"Good observations, though…they match my first impressions," Kittery said.

Then, because the trooper had been forthright with him, he added, "First time I saw a decapitated body was about 25 years ago…it was a high speed crash. The car went under the back of a trailer."

Mitch gave his own head a shake. "Bad business," he continued. "I took one look, turned around, and puked my guts out. To this day, the only way I can tell ya' that it was anything but a clean cut is to remember all the graphic news reports; it haunted me for months."

"Seems understandable," Russ said. "I puked the first time I saw a highway fatality. I know this one's gonna keep me awake all night tonight…probably all night for a month."

"If you are, just make sure it's your missus that you talk to about it, and not someone else." The burly sergeant shook his head, warning, "A man can get himself into a lot of trouble without even meaning for it to end that way."

Russ had a feeling the man on the other side of the long table was speaking from personal experience, but let it pass, saying only, "Thanks for the advice, Sergeant…I lost my wife a couple years back, but I'll remember it."

"Call me Mitch," the man across the table said.

"Thank you," Russ said. "It was tough out there this morning, Mitch, I'll admit it…'course I wasn't alone when I found the body. Barnaby Moss was with me, and it helped."

A slightly self-conscious smile appeared on the trooper's lips when he admitted, "I didn't wanna puke in front of a witness…especially when he was keeping it together."

With one bushy brow cocked higher than the other, the veteran officer commented, "I noticed there was no vomit on the ground, when I was having my first look see at the site." Giving Russ a tension-breaking grin, he added, "I was surprised about that, I'll tell ya' the truth."

In the course of his career, Mitch Kittery had seen law enforcement officers lose last week's lunch for less than a decapitation—himself included. It was almost impossible to look at a mangled mess, barely recognizable as human, without praying to God that the horror settling in the pit of your stomach could be retched out.

"Believe me," Russ said, "I was swallowing pretty hard. I looked back at the Moss kid…well, he's not actually a kid, he's 25…"

"But that's still a kid to us," Mitch chuckled as he interrupted.

Russ nodded his head quickly, and said, "I never thought I'd see the day when someone 25 would look like a boy to me, but I've gotten there."

In the last two years since losing Phyllis, and especially in the eight months when she had battled the cancer that finally claimed her life, he had felt far older than a man in his 40s—sometimes he felt 90.

Shifting again in his seat, both from the physical discomfort, and the thought of his beloved wife, Russ continued, "Anyhow, when I walked back to him, and asked if he was

OK, he said he was…he was pretty damned white, and shaking like hell, but if he said he was OK, I wasn't gonna argue the point with him."

Mitch looked back over his notes. Thumbing to the page he wanted, he read it back, and then said, "He's a recording engineer? Music business must be tough, if he could take this without heaving his guts up."

The trooper's sudden grin was not in line with the topic, but he was impressed by the younger man's tenacity. "He might have wanted to, but that kid hung on—he even managed to take a second look to confirm that it was Gloria Baines." Russ could still see Barn talking himself into taking a longer look at the disembodied face. He might be gay, but he was no less a man.

"So you even got us a positive ID…nice work, Russ," Kittery said.

With his pen poised over his notebook again and his eyes boring directly into the intelligent eyes of the trooper, Kittery asked, "Anyone in particular give you a bad feeling, Russ?"

Johnson nodded, "I'll tell you straight out that I don't like Sydney Slating, and I never have been able to stand George Parker, the innkeeper here. Bastard beat his wife, but I could never nail him, because she wouldn't press charges…go figure."

He slapped his hand down on the desk with such force, that Mitch knew the reaction was personal.

"Do you have a reason to think he had something to do with this, Russ, or is it just a personal feeling?" Kittery asked, already knowing the answer.

Johnson shook his head, and answered, "Mostly personal, I guess, but that doesn't say he's not a rotten son of a bitch with a history of violence against women."

He was clearly passionate about this subject, and concluded, "The days when a man could beat his wife, but only with a certain size stick, have been gone for a long time."

"I'm not proposing legislation to bring that ordinance back, Russ. Simmer down," Kittery said. "Where's the wife now?"

"Dead...had a heart attack last summer."

"OK, then, let's move on from there, all right?" The reprimand was gentle; Kittery wanted more pertinent information, but he would not forget the trooper's words.

Russ nodded, "Sorry, I should know better than to bring unrelated matters into an investigation; Bessie Parker was my wife's aunt."

Kittery nodded, and put a star near Parker's name. Just because the other man's reason for disliking Parker was personal, did not mean it was not justifiable. Violence was violence.

"I did do one other thing right after discovering the body," Johnson said.

"What's that?"

"I called the headquarters first, of course, but then I went across to the White Star Tavern. I'd just been over there this morning fixing the door on the Grissom's tool shed… Gretchen Grissom called me the other morning, and said she thought she'd heard someone around the shed the night before…Sunday night…"

"Door busted before then?" Kittery interrupted, his ears perking up.

"Yes, apparently, but Whit Grissom, Gretchen's husband, just hadn't gotten around to calling me." Feeling the need to explain why he was doubling as a handyman, he added, "I do a lot of fix-up carpentry work around here in my less busy hours."

Kittery smiled at the trooper. Up here, things usually were pretty quiet. "A good day's work doesn't need to be justified, Russ," he said, in an almost paternal way, before asking, "Did you ask 'em if anything was missing from the shed…an axe maybe?"

"Yes, sir…Gretchen came right out for a look see, but it took Whit a little while to get his ass in gear…."

"Older people, are they?"

"She's in her mid-60s…he's about 70, I guess. He's in pretty good shape, though. He had a bypass last summer, but he's doing well for his age. She's a pistol."

"OK," Kittery said. "I just wanted to get a picture of 'em in my head…go on…anything missing?"

"Gretchen said nothing was missing, and she's the one who chops the firewood…really fusses over him since the bypass, she does."

Nodding, Kittery said, "Sounds like a normal wife, but at her age, she shouldn't be chopping wood; she'll be the next one in the hospital, pistol or not."

"Suppose so," the trooper agreed, "but she does it anyway. I lend her a hand when she calls me, but she doesn't always do that."

His comment reminded him of George Parker again, and he said, "She watches George Parker all the time; she knows how he was to his wife. I swear if the man looks sideways at her, I hear about it within minutes. Come to think of it, she's got Barn and his buddy, Arnie, keeping an eye on him now. She told 'em she gets real worried about women staying alone over there."

Mitch added the new information to the page where George Parker's name was already starred. Taking the discussion back to the whereabouts of the axe, he said, "So, about the axe…he's sure one was missing? If she chops the wood, I'd think she'd know."

"Yeah, I've been thinking about that myself," Russ replied. "I'm thinking now that there could've been a time when Whit did more than he does now…larger axe could've been from back then. He described it as having a rusty head the last time he saw it…"

"Sounds like a good chance that he hadn't seen it in a long time then," Kittery interrupted.

Nodding his head emphatically, he added, "Could be the wife just never saw the thing…that happens. I doubt my wife could tell you everything I've got out in our shed."

Grinning, he admitted, "Shit, sometimes, even I couldn't." Returning to the point, he asked, "Get a description of it… aside from the rusty head?"

Russ answered, "Old coot's really a charmer. When I asked him to describe it, he said, 'It looks like an axe, you jackass'…but then he did condescend to tell me it had a red handle."

Kittery theorized, "Missing axe is probably our murder weapon…I'll get the crime scene people to comb the woods around the place for an axe matching his sterling description."

After making a note about that directive on his pad, he looked back at the trooper, and said, "Now, Russ, tell me what it is you dislike about Sydney Slating."

"Nothing personal there, Mitch," Russ replied. "From all accounts, Slating made a point of running the dead woman's character down just yesterday morning, and he did the same thing this morning when I talked to him. I didn't much like that. He acted like this woman was a substance-abusing hooker, but he had only just meet her… that's not normal."

He hesitated for just long enough to draw another breath, before saying, "His sister told me that he's down on women, especially redheads, since his divorce—from a redhead. Jane, the sister, was pretty mad at him for the way he'd acted at breakfast the other morning…"

"Play one witness off another very often?" Kittery interrupted.

Russ laughed, "Sometimes…but it wasn't like that this morning. She offered the information freely. I'll raise my hand and admit it's nothing concrete. I didn't see anything specific that made me think he's involved, and she didn't say anything specific that would prove it. It's just that his attitude toward someone he'd probably spent less than an hour with, gave me a funny feeling."

Leaning forward across the table, Russ added, "There is one other thing. His sister mentioned hearing something during the night…she's the only one who did."

Mitch looked intently into the other man's eyes. "How'd she describe it?"

"Well, at first she said she didn't hear anything, but almost right away she added that it's an old place, and she heard the usual creaks…"

"But you don't think that was the case?" Mitch queried. He was impressed with Russ again; he was quick.

Russ shook his head. "It could have been, but the way she said it…I don't know…something just didn't feel right. It struck me that she might have been making a remark to dismiss a sound someone else might say they heard…I know she suspects her brother is involved. If I knew for sure what we were dealing with at that point, I would have pressed further."

A man who also trusted his gut instincts, Kittery responded, "I'll see what she says to me…good work, Russ."

He closed his notebook; it was time to move along to the second thing he needed to do this morning.

"Before I speak to everyone myself, I want to check a couple things. Did you think to get Social Security Numbers from everyone…not just their addresses and birth dates?"

"Right here" Johnson said, passing the state police officer his own notebook. "The personal information I took from everyone I talked to this morning is in all caps. The SSNs are underlined twice. Copy down what you need—or do you want me to do it for you?"

Kittery responded, "No…it's OK, Russ. I'll just take it out to the car."

"Doing a full background check on all of 'em right now?" Johnson asked.

"No, I'll leave that for when I'm back at headquarters. I want to get these interviews done, and have a closer look around outside. I'm just gonna run their names and numbers through the computer out in the car. I'll make sure everyone's who they say they are, and live where they say…nothing else right now."

He headed out to his vehicle.

Chapter 18

To the attorney seated in front of him, Mitch Kittery said, "You're from Texas, I see…"

Narrowing his pale blue eyes suspiciously, Slating said, "Why am I being asked this? I never saw that girl before breakfast yesterday. She seemed like a loose type to me; I told your trooper that."

'Hell with breaking the ice', Kittery silently fumed. The man's confrontational demeanor irritated him.

"He's not my trooper," he said, his voice slicing through the air. "If he'd been mine, he'd have asked you to account for every minute of your time today, from whenever you got outta bed, to the minute you dragged your skinny butt back in here this morning…where were you, Mr. Slating?"

"None of your damned business where I was…"

Kittery cut him off with a voice that clanged like the doorway to hell.

"Everything here is my business, if I think it is, Slating," he barked. "My crime scene people could play 1-on-1 with that young woman's head. I'm gonna start ruling suspects out, or I'm gonna start rounding 'em up. What's it gonna be for you, Slating? Are you gonna talk to me here, or are you gonna talk to me at headquarters up in Mill River?"

Slating screwed up his already unpleasant face, but answered the question. "My sister and I ate out last night, and I went right to bed afterwards."

"Where did you eat?" Kittery snapped, his voice not even one decibel lower.

Slating pursed his thin lips together in apparent disgust. "In Mill River…the 'Orange Acorn'. Stupid name for a restaurant, if you ask me."

"I didn't," Kittery growled. "What did you eat?"

"Steak…rare and overpriced," Slating said snidely.

Mitch Kittery understood Russ Johnson's feelings; this was a horrendous first date, and they were still on the appetizer.

"How long were you there?" he asked.

"I don't know."

"Any idea what time you got home?" Kittery said, suddenly struck by the pleasant vision of beating Sydney Slating with a rubber hose.

"Before eight o'clock."

Kittery got uglier than he normally would have; even difficult witnesses usually did not get under his skin. Slating was already sitting on his bare bones. "Did you sleep with your sister, or did you sleep alone?"

The way Sydney Slating shot out of his chair, an observer would have suspected George Parker of installing ejector seats.

"What did you say to me?" the scrawny lawyer shouted. His eyes were wild with rage. "How dare you accuse me of fucking my own sister?"

Forcing his voice to remain absolutely level, and even to sound puzzled by Slating's outburst, Kittery asked, "Who said anything about fucking your sister? I asked if slept alone."

"You asked if I slept with my sister."

"I meant in the same room," Kittery said, all innocence.

Slating sat back down and controlled his temper, but it was clearly a struggle.

"My sister and I are sharing one of the back rooms; it's got twin beds, and right between 'em there's a divider that pulls out from the wall."

"Can your sister verify that you were in that bed all night long?"

"I can't answer questions for my sister. Ask her."

"I'm asking you...what do you think, Slating? If you left the room for any reason, say to walk down the hall and stretch your legs, would your sister have been disturbed?"

Slating was making this interview a lot harder than it needed to be. "I don't know."

"Slating, this is a simple enough question. To get out of that room, would you have had to pull that folding divider back at all, or is the door to the hallway on your side of the room?"

In a rare moment of cooperation, Slating answered, "I'd have had to pass Jane's bed to get to the door. My sister's a fairly light sleeper, and that damned divider gizmo makes a racket; if I left, she'd have woken up."

"Thank you, Mr. Slating."

"You're entirely welcome, I'm sure," Slating drawled.

Kittery glared at the Texan. "Is there a window on your side of the room?" he demanded.

"Yes...but I already wiped off my fingerprints after I climbed out."

With a vague thought about the phrase 'justifiable homicide' drifting through his mind, Kittery leaned forward across the table. "Smart mouth me again in the course of my investigation, Slating, and I'll bust your sorry ass. Got that?"

Slating got two stars placed after his name...and they were not because he was a good boy in class.

> <

Kittery began his next interview with the words, "It's been a terrible day so far, Ms. Slating."

"Jane, please," the new witness said.

Kittery thought this Slating sibling looked like a pleasant person—certainly nicer than her brother—but the nervous twisting of her fingers in her lap told the sergeant that she was scared. Still, she gave him a pleasant smile, and looked to be nothing but cooperative.

He began again, "Jane, I've already verified the personal information you gave to the trooper this morning, at least your name, address and Social Security Number."

Making a small joke to lessen her fears, he said, "I checked your date of birth too, but I won't make it a matter of public record."

His remark had the desired effect. Jane Slating smiled at him, and said, "That's OK, 45 isn't such a bad age."

"I liked it myself," Kittery smiled at his witness. "It's better than 57," he said. "Now, getting down to business, Jane, did you know Gloria Baines before this trip?"

"No, sir...I never met her until yesterday morning," the woman responded. "We saw the car in the lot, so we knew there were other guests in the house, but we never met either of the girls until breakfast yesterday. Until this morning, I didn't even know which room they were in...they've been very quiet."

She shrugged, and added, "After we realized Gloria was missing, Lizzie became very upset, and the innkeeper told me to take her up to her room. The poor girl was so frightened, and crying her head off..."

Suddenly realizing what she had just said, Jane clapped her hands over her mouth for a minute. Her next words, "I didn't mean to say that," were followed by a sudden, and obviously unexpected, outburst of tears.

"Please, forgive me," she said to the burly sergeant only a moment later. "I'm not usually a bundle of nerves like this, but you were quite right. It has been a terrible day so far."

She produced a tissue from the sleeve of her sweater, and dabbed first her eyes, and then her turned-up nose.

Kittery gave her a few seconds longer to regain her composure before asking, "Where were you last evening, Jane?"

"Sydney and I ate at the 'Orange Acorn' last night..." Jane began, a slight tremor coming into her voice. She understood immediately that he was asking her to verify her brother's alibi.

"We went out early, and were home before eight o'clock. My brother went right up to bed, but I stayed down here for a time."

Kittery asked, "Do they still have that great lobster pie on the menu? My wife and I always order it when we're there...but we haven't been there in a couple months."

"I can't say as I recall seeing it on the menu...I could have missed it..."

Kittery chuckled, patting his stomach, "Just as well if they cut it," he joked, "I think it's put 15 pounds on me."

He looked down at his notes again, and then said, "So you were back here by eight o'clock, and your brother went right up to bed?"

"Yes sir, that's right," Jane answered. "I settled down at the table here to look at the paper. Barn came in not too long after that; I'd seen he and his friend going out with the two girls after breakfast, so I asked where the rest of them were. He said Arnie and Lizzie went to the movies, and Gloria was still over at the tavern, but he was going up to bed."

Jane paused, wishing she had gone straight upstairs with Sydney; because she had lingered to read the paper, she now had the surprisingly daunting task of verifying the time when everyone else got back to the inn last night.

She continued, "Gloria walked in at about ten o'clock; she seemed quiet...much more so than at breakfast...so I asked her if everything was all right. She said that she was just tired, and went straight upstairs."

Jane sighed, and continued to verify the time of everyone's return to the inn. "Mr. Parker, the owner, came in just after Gloria. He was muttering under his breath...something about 'damned old bag, who's she think she is closing up early'...something like that." She smiled slightly, and added, "I guess he wasn't done drinking."

More seriously, she said, "At first, he went right into the kitchen, but then he came back in here saying he wanted to watch TV, so I went up to the room."

"Did you hear the others come in?" Kittery asked. He had not expected to come this far so fast, but Jane was a very good witness; her details were clear and concise, and she wasted no time telling them.

"Yes, I did. It was probably not long before 11," she said. "I had taken a quick shower, and just gotten into bed, when I heard them out in the hallway…they said goodnight, and went to their rooms."

Making his notes, Kittery nonchalantly said, "I'd guess that, if your brother's like me, he woke right up when you came out of the bathroom…I swear, I can hear Marge thinking about opening that door."

"No, he didn't wake up."

Forearmed, thanks to Russ' earlier comment, Mitch was ready to find out if she could verify that her brother was in bed…maybe the bathroom door did not disturb him because he was not there to be disturbed. With a seemingly friendly chuckle, he said, "Didn't miss a snore, huh?"

Jane Slating smiled. "Syd doesn't snore," she said.

'Interesting', Mitch silently mused. 'I don't know any more now than I did a minute ago…maybe he really doesn't snore.' Directly he asked, "Are you sure he was in the room?" To himself he thought, 'and not out checking on the axe he took from Grissom's shed the night before?'

Unless he missed his guess, his pretty witness had been expecting that question.

Shaking her head, Jane answered, "No, I don't suppose I am. There's a divider between the beds, if you aren't already aware of it. I didn't go around it to look at him." Pausing for only the briefest instant, she added, "I think I'd have heard the divider being pulled back, if it was pulled back, but I don't know for sure. All I do know for sure is that he was in the room this morning."

It had not been an easy answer for her to give, but Jane Slating was an honest woman.

"Fair enough," Mitch said. "Did you hear anyone in the hall during the night?"

"No, I don't think so," Jane answered. "Just the house settling, I suppose" she added, in the same hurried voice she had used in relaying the information to the state trooper.

She was terrified that her brother made the noise she heard; she wanted Mitch to ask about it, but she did not want to offer the information directly.

Mitch looked up, as Russ had done earlier, and he understood why his colleague felt the way he did. Jane Slatting looked very worried.

"What time, Jane?" he asked the anxious woman. "You heard something. Tell me about it."

Clenching and unclenching her small hands, Jane answered, "I think I had been asleep for a little while…maybe it was after midnight, but I don't really know. It was the softest sound. It could've been the house creaking, but, ever since I heard about the note this morning, and realized Gloria was…ah…gone, I've wondered if the house creaked alone."

Her eyes met Kittery's. They showed fear—they also showed determination. "If you want to know if I'm worried that my brother may've put the note under the door across the hall" she said, "yes, I am. Sometimes I feel like I don't know who he is anymore."

Looking back through the notes he had made when speaking to Russ Johnson earlier, Kittery said, "Your brother has no history of violence." It was a statement, not a question.

"No sir," Jane answered. Smiling in a way that said she was embarrassed by the thought, she said, "Sydney was always such a…well…a wimp, that I wondered for a lot of years if he was…" She deliberately let her voice trail away, and shrugged; what she had wondered was obvious.

Not unkindly, Kittery said, "Homosexuality has nothing to do with a person's courage."

Jane nodded. "I know…but it's what I thought at the time."

Kittery acknowledged the statement with a shake of his own head, and then steered the interview back to last night by asking, "You didn't open your door to check out the noise, though?"

"No, sir," Jane answered. "At the time, I had no reason to think it was anything more than an old house settling. I just went back to sleep."

He moved on to his next question. "Which one of you was awake first this morning?"

"Actually, I think we woke up at about the same time," Jane responded. "I wanted to use the bathroom, but Syd wanted to get out and take his walk, so I let him go in first. He's generally in the habit of going out earlier, but this morning he didn't leave until just before eight o'clock."

"Hear any unusual noises in the hallway this morning?"

"I heard the door across the hall open and close, and then heard footsteps descending the stairs. I realize now that it must have been Gloria, but, at the time, I didn't look out; there was nothing else out of the way."

"No other footsteps on the stairs except hers?"

"No, not until Sydney left."

"Thank you, Jane. This hasn't been easy for you, I'm sure, but you've been very helpful."

Jane Slating's interview yielded her a check mark after her name. If she had anything to do with this, Kittery was a ballerina.

Chapter 19

Eyes red and hands shaking, Lizzie Tidman took a seat, and avoided making eye contact with her new interrogator.

"Tell me what happened this morning, Ms. Tidman... Lizzie."

"I don't know, exactly" she answered, looking at the table.

Already, Kittery had a sense of something being wrong; it was not only that she was so nervous he would have to walk her through her own testimony...it was the way she was deliberately not making eye contact. What was she afraid he would see?

"What time did you wake up?"

"A little after seven, I guess...before 7:30."

"Were you alone in the room?"

"Oh, no, no, Gloria was still there…we didn't talk, but she was there. I went in to take a shower, and she came barging in on me not terribly long after that. She said she'd just noticed a note from Barney, and she was going downstairs to meet him."

Looking up for a fleeting second, Lizzie asked, "You do know about the note, right?"

"Yes."

Without warning, she started to cry; Kittery was not a tough talking but softhearted TV detective who just happened to carry a bunch of tissues in his pocket for moments like these. He pulled a few paper napkins from the wooden napkin holder on the table, and passed them to his second weeper of the day.

"Tell me what happened after you'd finished showering," he said. "You thought Gloria left. Did you go right downstairs…what did you do?"

Wiping her eyes, the witness continued, "I got dressed, and went right downstairs, yes. It was just after eight o'clock, I guess. Jane Slating was already sitting at the table, and her brother was just going out the door. Jane and I sat at the table together, just making small talk. Right now, I don't even remember what we were talking about. I heard the guys coming downstairs, and thought I must be hearing wrong. I knew Sydney Slating had gone out, and I thought Gloria and Barney had too…"

Looking past Kittery's head and out the window, Lizzie asked, "What else do you want to know?"

"Why, Lizzie? Is there something more you want to tell me?" Kittery asked in his 'fatherly' voice. He was not sure why he had asked the question—it seemed to form itself.

"No," Lizzie answered adamantly. "Nothing. That's all I know." Tears streaked her cheeks again, and her shoulders shook with sobs; there would be no more she could tell him right now.

Kittery released her for the moment, but the feeling that there was something else the young woman desperately wanted to get off her chest stayed with him.

He put a star after her name.

> <

Arnold Kotkin shook hands with Kittery before taking a seat to tell the exact same story he had related to Russ Johnson just hours earlier.

Kittery expected nothing less from the young man; Russ Johnson's notes indicated that Kotkin seemed to have a good head on his shoulders, and was extremely observant.

The only thing Johnson had not found out about the post-grad student was that he had attempted suicide at the beginning of the year. He admitted it candidly at the end of the interview with Kittery, when, closing his notebook, the sergeant asked, "Is there anything else you think I should know about?"

"Well, it has nothing to do with this, but if you do any checking, you'll find out anyway, so I'll tell you myself... I made a suicide attempt last New Year's Eve."

He looked directly into Kittery's eyes as he spoke. "I would've told Trooper Johnson" he added, "but it just didn't come up in the conversation...I wasn't trying to hide it."

"Why did you try to kill yourself?" Kittery was surprised by the news; Kotkin seemed to be as calm and in control as any person he had ever met.

"It was a combination of things," Arnie explained. "My father had a slight heart attack, and that same night, my friend, Barn, got shot...I don't know if it ever made the news up here, but it was all over the papers back in New York." He raised an eyebrow, asking for confirmation with the simple expression.

"No...at least if it did, I never heard about it," Mitch Kittery said. "If you feel I should know about it, tell me."

Looking steadily into two of the greenest eyes he had ever seen, Arnie continued with a nod, "Well, I need to, in order to explain the suicide attempt."

"Go ahead, then." Kittery sat back to listen. He doubted that he would need to make any notes on this.

"After the shooting, and all the media mess, I got suspended from my job; I was a science teacher," Arnie said. "I did tell the trooper that I had been a teacher, but I'm back in school now, working toward my doctorate."

"You got suspended over media innuendo?" Kittery asked.

"Pretty much," Arnie answered. "Even though I got reinstated almost right away, things were so bad that I ended up resigning; it's a long story. Anyway, a couple days before I handed in my resignation, my younger brother was killed in a car accident."

He shook his tawny head, summarizing, "It was just one thing after another. I'll give you all the details if you want them, but they really have no bearing on anything that's happened up here…just on why I tried to kill myself."

Kittery knew the young man's suicide attempt ten months earlier had nothing to do with the mess he had seen outside this morning, but as a law enforcement officer, and a man who had long believed the news media to be a two-edged sword at times, he wanted to get all the details anyway. He placed a star near his name.

"No, that's not necessary," he told the former teacher. "I can check it out later, if I need to."

"Is that all?"

Kittery glanced back at his notes. "Yes, I think that's about it…just send Barnaby Moss downstairs, all right?"

"You've got him," Arnie said, as he rose to leave the room.

> <

"Hi," Barnaby Moss said, bouncing down the stairs and walking toward the table. "Arnie said you're ready for me."

Kittery stood up, and extended a hand to the young engineer. Barn grasped it, and, to Kittery's surprise, he had a good grip. "If you're Barnaby Moss, I'm ready for you," he said.

For the second time that day, Barn sat down in the straight-backed chair that was serving as the witness stand.

Skipping the breakfast conversation from yesterday morning entirely, Kittery asked, "Do you remember if George Parker was in the room when Ms. Tidman made her announcement about finding the note?"

Kittery had not asked anyone that question yet, but he had not forgotten Johnson's admitted dislike and distrust of the man.

He would interview him soon, and wondered if anyone could place George Parker in the room when the note was brought to light, and cast doubt on the possibility that he might have been somewhere else trying to wash blood off of his clothes and body.

Barn thought for a second, and said, "I think he was behind the table….yeah, he was. He was just giving Jane Slating a cup of coffee when we were coming down the stairs."

"OK," Kittery said. He did not ask the youthful engineer about the note either. The state police officer had heard essentially the same story from everyone else he had asked; it was unlikely that the young man watching him with curious, dark eyes from across the table would suddenly contradict everyone else, and say 'just kidding—I wrote it'. Instead, he said, "You were with Russ Johnson when he found the body, and made a positive ID?"

"Yeah…it was Gloria," Barn answered.

"OK," Kittery said, and then, backtracking, said, "When I talked to Russ Johnson a little earlier, he said you had mentioned to him that the two young women had words yesterday when you were out. Can you tell me about that?"

Kittery sat back, and listened to a retelling of the story Barn had already related to Russ Johnson.

When he finished speaking, he surprised the sergeant with a question he had not expected to hear. "Could a woman have done this?"

"Are you thinking of Lizzie Tidman?" Kittery asked in reply.

Barn drummed his fingers lightly on the edge of the table, shaking his head. "I don't wanna be, but who else up here would've done it? Chopping somebody's head off is kinda personal."

"It could be done, I'd say," Kittery said. "One clean whack; the human neck isn't made of steel. You saw the body. It was face down, so to speak," he said, feeling the way Jane Slating must have felt earlier when she had made the comment about Lizzie crying her head off.

He wasted no time choosing new words, but continued with, "When I saw the body, my first thought was that whoever did this, came up behind her…"

"She'd have put her hands up otherwise," Barn interrupted, quickly grasping the sergeant's meaning.

"Exactly," Kittery said. "She would've put them up automatically to shield her face…and we'd have two severed hands out in the grass too." He nodded his head resolutely, and said, "No question in my mind that a woman could have done this."

Barn opened his mouth to speak again, but he never got the words out, because the sergeant unexpectedly asked, "How's the gunshot wound?"

"Arnie told you about that?" he responded, the words he had intended to say were forgotten for the second time that day.

"He said you'd been shot; he told me about his suicide attempt, too…you find him?"

None of this had any bearing on the brutal slaying that morning, and Kittery knew it, but he felt compelled to ask—if nothing else, it would explain how this kid held it together, when anyone else could reasonably have been expected to toss the contents of their stomachs onto the unkempt parking lot.

"Yeah, I did. He slit his wrists in our bathtub; he did a crappy job of it, thank God, but he still lost a lot of blood… the place was a mess."

Briefly taking his eyes away from Kittery's, Barn looked out the window, seeing, but not really concentrating on, the activity outside.

When he continued to speak, he again made eye contact with the sergeant. "I left work early, and found him when I got home. It was a bad…pretty much the whole year before that was bad," he said, heaving a deep sigh. "Neither one of us handled the stress particularly well, although we pretended to for a long time."

Like all the other witnesses who had come into the room, he shifted uncomfortably in the chair. He was the only one to make a comment about it, though. Grinning, he said, "I think this guy got the most uncomfortable chairs he could find…probably makes people leave the table faster."

Kittery smiled at the remark, and then said, "Arnie offered to give me all the details, but they don't have any bearing on what I'm here to investigate, so I declined to hear them…just for my own curiosity, though, where were you shot?"

Barn assumed the sergeant was trying to determine whether or not swinging an axe was a physical impossibility for him.

"Up here" he said, reaching up to touch the spot with his right hand. "The bullet caught me just here, right under my collarbone. I guess it went in on a little bit of an angle, because it exited between my shoulder blade and my spine, without doing anything other than nerve and muscle damage—but there was a lot of that."

Letting his right hand rejoin the left one in his lap, the young man offered a friendly smile, and added, "It still bugs me." Shaking his dark head, he added, "I don't have a full range of motion anymore…and it gets numb a lot…"

"Does it interfere with your work?" Kittery interrupted.

"Yeah, sometimes," the height challenged engineer admitted. "I'm finally learning to deal with it, but I got pretty frustrated with it last year; it was tough to be at the consol in the control booth, and have my fingers go numb on me when I was riding the dials."

After a brief pause, Kittery asked, "Who shot you?"

Flashing a quick grin as he realized Kittery really was just curious, Barn responded, "Arnie's brother...but, listen, if you want the whole story, I've got time; I don't have to be anywhere specific until Wednesday at two o'clock."

Kittery laughed, slapping both hands down on the table, "Kid," he said, "I started out just trying to figure out how you kept from puking out there...finding your friend after he'd cut his wrists, accounts for it, and that's saying nothing about your own injury."

Glancing out the window again, Barn said, "There was a lot of coverage; probably **The Daily Reporter** was more accurate than anyone else, and even they got a little nasty. I don't remember the exact date...I've managed to forget it...but it was at the end of last April."

He imagined that, when this case was wrapped up, Kittery would be spending some time online, trying to locate the old stories.

"What's two o'clock Wednesday, by the way?" Mitch Kittery asked, suspecting he knew exactly what it was.

"I'm getting married." Barn answered simply.

Leaning back in his own highly uncomfortable chair, Kittery nodded, and said, "I suppose it makes sense to go ahead with it—you've come all this way—but it's gonna make it hard for you to forget this date."

"Probably," Barn answered without hesitation, "but, like you said, we drove all the way up." This time being biologically correct, he added, "Plus, Arnie's parents drove up to be our witnesses."

This was entirely new information; Kittery had heard nothing about a Mr. and Mrs. Kotkin being here. "I didn't know that," he answered.

"You must have," Barn responded, "They got here this morning, and saw all the flies outside. It was Dr. Fentnor who told Russ Johnson about it."

Quickly jumping to the assumption that Arnie Kotkin was the child of Helene Fentnor's first marriage, Kittery said, "Oh, yes, I did hear about them. I didn't realize…ask 'em to come on down for a second, would ya'?"

Thinking that it had been the Fentnors bad luck to see all the flies from the North Atlantic seaboard gathered together for a morning's feast, Kittery also thought that

Arnie's mother and step-father had found the body; they had just been fortunate enough not to see it.

> <

In response to the sergeant's inquiry, Jack Fentnor said, "I'm Dr. Jonathan Fentnor, and I'm an oral surgeon. I live with my wife, Helene, and our daughter, Emily, in Litchfield, Connecticut."

He graciously supplied the rest of the routine personal information when Kittery requested it.

When she was asked for the same information, Helene Fentnor, a stunningly beautiful woman, whose son greatly resembled her, provided it willingly.

In response to Kittery's question about her occupation, the wife of a man so wealthy he could buy New England, answered, "I'm a housewife and mother."

Her answer provided Kittery with the perfect opening for his next question. "Barnaby Moss told me you're up here to serve as witnesses for them at their marriage Wednesday. Arnie seems to be a fine young man, Mrs. Fentnor. He's from your first marriage, I take it."

The housewife from Litchfield smiled, and shook her blond head. "No," she answered forthrightly, as her husband grinned broadly at her. "He's from when Jack and I were just teenagers…my sister and her husband adopted him, but we're still his natural parents."

Kittery liked her; he imagined some women might not have owned up to that one straight off the bat. "I should know better than to assume," he laughed. "Sorry, Doctor, I didn't mean to slight you."

"Quite all right," Jack said, smiling. "He acts more like me, but he looks like his mother."

Bringing the subject back to the investigation at hand, Kittery asked, "I already know you saw the flies outside this morning when you arrived. Did you notice any part of the body at all?"

He asked the question, even though Barnaby Moss said the Fentnors had only reported seeing the flies; it was not unusual for a witness to remember details only briefly glimpsed, if they were asked the right question.

Considering the question, and forcing his mind back to the moment when he eased his car into a grassy parking spot, Jack answered, "I remember seeing what looked like a wall of flies over by the edge of the parking lot…that was even before we got out of our car. After I'd gotten out, I looked over again."

His eyes straining to see a sight no longer before them, but written instead on his memory, Jack said, "I half remember seeing something on the ground, something that, as much as all the flies, must have made me think a garbage can had been dumped over. I'm sure I didn't see what it actually was."

Helene spoke up. "That's the way I remember it, too... there was something on the ground, but it certainly didn't seem like a human shape. With all the flies around, a garbage can being dumped over seemed like a plausible explanation. It wasn't until we got inside, and Barn told us about the disappearance, that the flies seemed sinister. Jack told the trooper about it right away, and he and Barn ran outside."

Chapter 20

"Tell me where you were last night," Kittery began his interview with George Parker with an order, rather than a question.

Parker barked, "Over at that bitch's tavern from about 5:30 to a couple minutes before ten."

Clearly angry, he rambled on, "That battle-axe behind the bar closed the place early…I never go to that dump, unless I have to, but because I did, she closed up…I told her I knew she was just doin' it to get me outta there."

The sergeant had known the innkeeper for mere seconds, but he already found himself sympathizing with the 'battle-axe'. He asked, "Did anyone see you arrive home?"

"The Slating woman was sitting here at the table when I got back, so she can tell ya', if she hasn't already, what time I got back."

He had the ability to make a pleasant room dismal; the once sunny room suddenly seemed like a mausoleum.

"What did you do when you got back here?" Kittery asked him, already knowing that the highly disagreeable, rat-faced man before him had disappeared into his kitchen.

"What are you wasting my time for?" Parker asked, an insolent sneer marring the attractiveness of his rodent-like features.

He could not have cared less that a woman, a guest at his inn, had been beheaded near his parking lot just hours earlier. As far as he was concerned, he should be down at the service station now; he didn't have time to waste sitting here.

"Wasting your time, am I?" Kittery shot back. "Well, excuse me, Mr. Parker. Let me run out to the side yard there, and yell at that woman for getting her head chopped off…the fucking nerve of her to go getting herself killed just to waste your time!"

Punctuating every other word with a sharp bang on the table, he had George Parker bouncing around on his chair like a popcorn kernel down at the cinema; the sight amused him, despite his anger.

"Quit hopping, and start talking," he roared at the man.

George Parker, in the way of all bullies who are put in their place right away, complied. "I went out in the kitchen for awhile," he said. "I guess it was around 10:30 or so that I told her I wanted to watch some TV."

Defensively, he added, "There's TVs in all the rooms; they don't need to sit down here and bug me."

On a hunch, Kittery asked, "Did you see Lizzie, Gloria and the two young men who're staying here, over at the tavern?"

"I did."

"Was it crowed...did they see you?"

"Don't know if they saw me, and don't care."

Before Kittery could get on his case for his attitude again, he hurried on with his answer. "It was crowed, though... 'cept for Sunday nights, when it's quiet everywhere up here, the old bitch packs 'em in this time every year."

Gazing out the window overlooking the parking lot as though his eyes could miraculously hook a sudden turn and see the front of the property instead, he complained, "I see the cars parked all around the place...some of 'em park right on the green out front." He frowned, saying, "I could make a stink about that...I own that property..."

"You own the town green?"

Parker gave him a look that silently accused him of being slow on the uptake. "I never said it was the town green—town never said it either. Tourists assume it...think they can park there."

He rolled his beady eyes skyward, adding, "When Bessie, my late wife, was alive, she'd never let me complain about it; I don't bother now...it's not important to me anymore."

"I assumed it was municipal property myself," Kittery admitted, before resuming his line of questioning. "Getting back to your statement that you saw the young people in the tavern, did you see them leave?"

"The blonds left together sometime before eight o'clock, that would be Kotkin, and Lillie, no, Lizzie. Gloria, and the other guy, Barney Moss, stuck around for awhile."

"What time did they leave?"

"He left first—not too long after the other two, either." Snidely, he added, "Probably his kind tire easily..."

"Cut the crap, Parker," Kittery said firmly. Unlike Russ Johnson, Kittery was not going to let remarks slide just because the speaker was too stupid to know his ass from a hole in the ground. "Just tell me what time they left."

"Whatever," Parker said.

Kittery wished he could arrest him for the way he said the word. It was already a source of irritation to him, because he heard so many kids saying it on a daily basis. Amazingly, George Parker managed to pack even more indifference into it than the kids did. "What time did they leave?" he asked again.

"Moss left first...probably a couple hours before the redhead. She stayed at the bar with the hag. They were squawking away up there like crows, and screaming like banshees a couple times; running someone down, they were...probably me."

He closed his eyes, and shook his head, before saying, "I can't stand that damned old broad; if anyone ever does her in, come lookin' for me...the woman's an inferno busybody."

Kittery repressed a smile. He assumed the old man meant an eternal busybody and not a busybody who had burst into flames, but he did not ignore the man's other remarks; Russ Johnson might not be far off the mark. This guy was nuts.

"You said you don't go to the tavern often, Mr. Parker," he said. "Any special reason why?"

"Hate the bitch," Parker said flatly.

"So why were you there last night?" Kittery prompted.

"Because I wanted a beer, and I didn't have any. I stayed there talking to Myles Buck, my boss down at the service station; I work there part-time…generally about noon 'til, maybe, five o'clock."

"But you have been to the tavern before last night?" Kittery asked.

"Course I have," Parker said.

Scratching his bulbous nose, he began to impart some interesting information without prompting; Russ Johnson would have called it 'hanging himself without a rope', but Kittery thought of it as 'winding 'em up, and letting 'em go'.

"I don't go over there unless I absolutely have to," the innkeeper said. "Last night, I had to…I ran outta beer for the first time since Whit Grissom's heart attack a year ago."

Apparently warming to his story, Parker continued in a more conversational tone, "I went over that day after we…that's me and Bessie…saw all the emergency people around. I don't go any more than I have to, like I said. I can't stand the damned woman—she was always filling Bessie's head with foolishness."

"Foolishness?"

"Kept telling her she should leave me…we fought sometimes, and I raised my hand to her more than once."

George Parker's expression was bland; for all the emotion there, he could have announced that it was Tuesday.

"You beat your wife?"

Parked sighed. "Just said so," he answered, sounding bored.

"She's still living?" Kittery asked, already knowing the answer.

The innkeeper confirmed Russ Johnson's earlier remark. "No" he said, with no obvious regret, "she died last summer...heart attack."

Unbidden, he continued, "She died in the afternoon, I remember. Usually I'd have been down at the service station 'til suppertime, but for some reason...probably was real slow that day...I'd left early. When I got home, the ambulance was here; that battle-axe from the other side of the green called for 'em. She said later that she came over for tea, but I imagine it was just to bitch me out more."

"Because you beat your wife?" Kittery asked. He could not believe how indifferent the man seemed to his wife's death; the fact that he seemed to see nothing out of the ordinary in the fact that he had abused his wife, sent an icy finger racing toward Kittery's heart. For the first time, he thought he completely understood Russ Johnson's feelings.

"What else?" Parker said, and then added something that, in his eyes, cleansed him of the act. "It's not like I ever cheated on Bessie the way Whit Grissom did on that old hag he's hitched to…not that I blame him."

Irreverently, Kittery thought, 'funny how a routine decapitation can turn into a sex scandal'. He asked, "Whit Grissom has an eye for other women?"

"Yup," Parker confirmed. "First affair I knew of had to be over 20 years ago…and the old hag found out about it—caught 'em at it out back of the shed. She forgave him, but she still talks about it; every guest who's come through here since then has probably heard about it though her own lips."

"Doesn't sound too forgiving to me," Kittery noted; he had to remind himself that Whit Grissom was not the victim— Parker was supplying him with a lot of information that would make Gretchen Grissom look guilty, if Whit's head ever showed up on the chopping block.

"Nah, it's the truth," Parker continued. "I heard her telling Bessie about it one time. Afterwards, she said how he'd taken care of her dying parents early on, and she knew he didn't mean to cheat on her. She said it was just a moment of weakness…but there's been a lot more moments that she doesn't know about."

"Really?" Kittery thought it would be out of line to ask the witness to go get him a cup of coffee, but this story was getting good; it called for caffeine and a cigarette.

"Mind if I smoke?" he asked.

"Your lungs," Parker said. "Need coffee?"

"Ifit'snotrouble,"Kittery answered,suddenlyremembering a time when his mother had told him he should become a priest; right now, he thought it might have been worth it, just to hear the confessions.

"No trouble," Parker said. Normally, he would not have made the offer, but here was a chance to even the score with Gretchen.

He went to the kitchen, and returned to the table a short time later, a cup of black coffee in each hand. "Sugar and that dried creamer shit's still on the table," he said. "Spoons are there too."

"Go ahead with what you were saying," Mitch directed, getting his coffee ready to drink.

Parker resumed his tale, saying, "Whit had a heart attack last year…he didn't feel too good when he left here…"

"He got sick here?"

Parker nodded his grizzled head, and took a sip of his black coffee. "We didn't know he was here, at least not right away…guests are supposed to be out of their rooms by 11:30 in the morning…"

"What time was this?" Kittery asked, taking the first sip of his own coffee. It was lousy, but, with the cigarette he would soon light, he could get it down.

"Early afternoon…I don't remember what time, exactly," Parker answered. "Anyway, me and Bessie were in the kitchen…just sittin' at the table talkin' about stuff….and all of a sudden we heard the thumping, and the bed springs creaking—sounded like whoever it was had gotten about to the home stretch."

"Did you go up to investigate, or wait for him to…ah…finish?"

Kittery knew that was not the best choice of words, but it was too late to pick others. He took a long drag on the cigarette, and blew the smoke out slowly.

"I went up, but he'd already run his race; damned fool started having a heart attack as he got to the wire."

Parker shook his head, and, unbelievably, smiled at the memory. "Stupid bastard," he said, unwittingly using one of Gretchen's pet descriptions.

"You let him leave here without calling for help?" Kittery asked. He was not sure which man would win in a contest for lowest scum of the earth. Sydney Slating, George Parker and Whit Grissom all seemed to be genuine contenders for the title.

"We would've, we could see he was sick…he was pale, and his skin seemed kinda clammy looking," Parker explained indifferently, "but he refused to let us call. We didn't know it was a heart attack, not for certain. He said he could get home, and he'd call a doctor himself, if he needed to. We watched him 'til he got home, and he raised his hand to us when he got to the door…like saying he was OK."

Kittery scribbled the notes furiously, and then asked, "But he wasn't OK?"

"Nah, he ended up having a triple bypass…but he came through it good," George Parker said. "Bastard's still alive and cheatin'. I don't know where he meets up with 'em these days…he doesn't go many places but the tavern. I s'pose he could be seeing 'em someplace when he tells Gretchen he's going out for a walk in the afternoon."

Suddenly laughing, Parker said, "Horny old bastard would do it behind a tree, if he had to…already know he's done it behind the shed."

"He doesn't come over here anymore?" Kittery asked; without difficulty, he could imagine Parker collecting money from Whit Grissom for the privilege of using an upstairs room to have a go at some of his female guests… maybe that was part of what Gretchen Grissom was watching for; perhaps she was not as blissfully ignorant of her husband's indiscretions as Parker believed her to be.

"Not since that day," Parker answered. "I would'a thought nothing could make me feel sorry for the old bitch, but I did that day. She never closes the tavern, 'cept for holidays like Thanksgiving and Christmas, but she was sick that day. Just a cold, I think, but from what she told Bessie later on, she'd been out to the doctor's. Whit never would've opened the tavern on his own, so no one was inside when he went in there. When she got home, she found him on the floor; lucky for him she went into the tavern first, 'stead of goin' up the outside stairs to the second floor…he would'a died. Bessie never told the old hag that Whit'd been here…been sick when he left," George Parker concluded, shrugging indifferently.

"She never told Gretchen Grissom what happened?" Kittery asked, trying to understand what could motivate the innkeeper's late wife to keep her mouth shut about something like that…he knew Marge would have been yapping away on the phone in short order.

"No, neither of us did. Bessie didn't quite make it a whole year herself after that…if she had, it might've changed, but at the time, she didn't…she said it wasn't an easy position to be in. S'pose she just didn't know what to do, really."

Parker scratched his left ear, adding an unrelated thought. "I'll give the old hag that much, she loves Whit…she fusses over him like a mother hen since he had that bypass. You'd think he's the only man who ever had one. He doesn't have to lift a finger over there…she does everything."

If the day ever dawned when Gretchen Grissom learned her husband had been cheating on her for a quarter of a century, Kittery imagined he would be out here again.

Chapter 21

"Peanut, do you think we should go though with getting married tomorrow?" Arnie asked, gazing up at the discolored ceiling over their bed. The 'Honeybees 'n Raspberries Inn' really had seen better days.

Barn looked at his partner, settled beside him on the bed. They had both lain down after being questioned by Kittery—no point in staying downstairs.

They would cross the hall before too much longer and find out if the Fentnors wanted to go out for supper, but for now they were content to just lie on the bed, sometimes talking and sometimes cuddling together for the feeling of security it provided.

"Sergeant Kittery mentioned kind of the same thing to me," he answered, tacking on the question, "Why shouldn't we, babe?"

"Oh, I don't know," Arnie said, an uneasy edge coming into his voice. "Maybe just because we'd remember it every year."

Barn rolled onto his side, and draped an arm over his partner's chest. "Babe, if it was a personal friend who got killed, I'd probably agree, but..."

"But since it was only a guest from the same place, it's OK?" Arnie's voice was surprisingly sharp; the brutal slaying hit him harder than he realized, and his nerves were raw.

So far today, they had eaten nothing at all. The day had consisted entirely of giving statements, waiting to give more statements, and facing the sickeningly familiar 'this can't be happening' feeling.

"I didn't say that, Arnie, and I didn't mean for it to sound heartless, but it's true," Barn answered. "If she had been killed in a car accident, we'd still be planning to get married tomorrow..."

"You mean dead is dead?"

Barn rolled off of the bed, and turned quickly around to face his still-recumbent partner.

"Stop putting words in my mouth, Arnie. I'm the last one who's gonna be indifferent...I saw her, for Christ's sake! I nearly lost everything I'd eaten in the last month."

236

He was furious; to his own surprise, he was also on the verge of tears.

Contrite, Arnie said, "Barn, I'm sorry…I guess I forgot…"

"I didn't forget, damn it, and I'm not gonna forget…not ever…but I'm also not gonna let a murder that we had nothing to do with stop us from getting married tomorrow. I don't see why it should…"

He had to stop speaking; the emotions he had been fighting to control all day finally broke free. Throwing himself back down on the bed, he sobbed in helpless frustration and horror, as the hideous vision he had seen that morning burned into his mind.

Arnie wrapped his arms around his tiny friend, and drew him close. "I'm sorry, Barn…I'm sorry." He held his partner tightly to his chest for several minutes.

Barn finally pulled away, rolling to the edge of the bed, and swinging his legs over the side.

Taking one last quick swipe at his wet eyes, he cleared his throat and said, "From a practical standpoint, this is the only time we have right now. You'll have a long break, of course, but I won't."

He turned sideways to look at his partner, explaining, "I don't have any other vacation time until next summer. We've already gotten the license, your family's here. Come on, Arnie, let's still get married tomorrow." He clasped his hands together, appearing to pray.

Getting to his knees and crawling across the lumpy bed, Arnie knelt beside his partner and kissed the top of his dark head. "All right" he said softly, "but only because I can't stand to see you beg."

> <

The Orange Acorn was a tiny establishment situated on a woody lot not far off Route 5.

Pulling into the gravel drive, the occupants of the blue Lexus were all charmed by the small yard surrounding the restaurant. Trees dotted the property, each one garbed in a different shade of orange, and a weathered, wooden fence stood guard at the boundaries.

"This is what I think of whenever someone says 'Vermont'," Jack Fentnor said, pulling up the collar of his mohair sweater as he slid gracefully out of the Lexus.

The handsome, dark-haired oral surgeon had been looking forward to a short get-away just as much as his wife had. They had never left Emily for any length of time before, and both of the middle-aged parents knew they had to start doing that; she was nearly a year old.

For the rest of this week, while they were in Vermont with their grown son, their toddler daughter was having a get away of her own—Larry and Stella Moss had driven down to Connecticut yesterday to pick her up.

Helene climbed out of the passenger seat. "You don't think of opening the car door for your wife," she ribbed her husband, who had stopped near the front of the car, waiting for the other three to pile out.

The two backseat passengers laughed as they exited the luxury vehicle. "Does he usually get the door?" Arnie asked from right behind Helene.

Laughing pleasantly in the brisk, autumn wind as she turned to face the young man whose eyes matched her own, she said, "Oh, sometimes. He almost always did while I was pregnant…"

Jack quipped, "Your mother had a hard enough time just getting out of the car then, without the extra effort it took to actually open the door."

He knew the reaction would be swift, and it was—his wife's middle finger shot into the air like a rocket.

Laughing heartily, he led the way toward the entrance, making a great show of holding the door for Helene, while she pushed wind-blown, golden tresses away from her face.

As they stepped inside, all were struck by the room's simple elegance.

A dozen small, round tables, each one covered in pale orange linen, were set with white china, heavy silver, and sparkling crystal. Each table had as its centerpiece, a large cranberry candle covered with a clear glass chimney. A hand woven ring of bittersweet and dried flowers decorated the base of the glass flute.

The highlight of the room, quite intentionally, was the view through a large, sparkling clean, mullioned window set in the side of the small restaurant, opposite the entrance.

Not visible from the parking lot, the panorama caught all visitors by surprise; no one ever failed to be moved by the perfect country scene—an apple tree, currently resplendent in shades of amber, stood directly outside the large window, its branches low to the ground. Instinctively, everyone who saw it knew that over the years children and adults alike had climbed onto those branches and reached for the crunchy, red treats higher up.

To the delight of the small party, they were seated at a table right next to the window. Graciously, Arnie sat with his back to the window. Barn sat opposite him, with Helene to his right, and Jack to his left.

Their waitress appeared with a large pitcher of water almost the moment the hostess placed their menus on the table. "Evening, I'm Jenny," she said, pouring water for each of the people at the table, and favoring each one with a friendly smile. "Can I start you folks off with a cocktail?"

Never a big drinker, Helene had even given up wine during her pregnancy, and had not gotten back into the habit of having a glass either before or after dinner. "Just a ginger ale for me, please," she answered.

"That will work for me, too," Jack replied.

Smiling across the small, linen-covered table at his wife, the handsome man said, "Our first time away without the baby, and this is how we celebrate. Do we know how to live, or what?"

Barn, stomach feeling queasy from the day's events, asked, "Can I have a glass of milk?"

"Sure can, hon," the blue-eyed Jenny answered, smiling brightly at the man she assumed to be a pre-teen. "Chocolate or regular?"

"Regular's fine," Barn answered, his voice soft.

Seated across the table from his mini-mate, Arnie grinned and said, "I'll have whatever's on tap."

"OK, be right back," Jenny said. Dropping pen and pad into the roomy pocket of her muskmelon-colored apron, she set off in the direction of the kitchen, brown ponytail bouncing on her neck.

Jack, with a smile stretching across his face, looked at the young man beside him, and said, "What...no Heineken tonight, 'hon'?"

"Nah...it's the day," Barn answered. "I saw way too much today."

Taking a sip from the crystal water goblet before him, he added, "Some people drink when they're upset, and think it makes 'em feel better...I know it's a momentary illusion. I'm better off with the milk. It might settle my stomach a little."

Immediately, Jack responded, "Barn, I'm sorry. I shouldn't have teased you...."

The object of Jack's pang of guilt cut in, "No, Dr. Fentnor, its OK...no apology's necessary." He picked up his menu, and began to study it, gradually becoming aware that Arnie was watching him.

Looking up to meet the hazel eyes of his partner, he said, "Problem?"

Arnie shook his head, and confessed, "No, I just thought of something...do you remember hearing Gloria and Lizzie starting to have another argument at that antiques store yesterday?"

Dropping his menu abruptly down onto the orange surface of the table, Barn said, "Shit, I was gonna say something to Russ Johnson, but then he asked me another question before I could, and we never got back to it."

Reaching for his water glass again, he added, "Same thing happened with Kittery now that I think of it. Right after I asked him if a woman could've done this..."

"You asked him that?" Arnie said, the hand that held his own water goblet frozen in the air.

Nodding his dark head sharply, Barn answered, "Yeah, I'd mentioned the quarrel they had in the car to Russ Johnson, and then I repeated it to Kittery—by the way, he says a woman could've done this. I was all set to say they'd had more than one argument the day before, but, again, I never got the words out, because all of a sudden he asked me how my gunshot wound was..."

Chewing his lower lip in apparent angst over his partner's missed opportunities, as well as his own forgetfulness, Arnie interrupted, "So the authorities don't know about the second fight at all. I can't believe I totally forgot about it until now—at least you thought of it..."

"For all the good it did," Barn cut in quickly.

Seated quietly throughout the partners' brief exchange, Jack and Helene's eyes had bounced back and forth like tennis balls at Forrest Hills.

Finally, Jack asked the obvious question, "Working on a theory?"

Barn shook his head. "I don't know, really. It's just that the two of them were fighting a couple times yesterday…what we heard wasn't worth killing someone over…"

"But who knows what we might not have heard," Arnie interjected quickly. "I wish one of us had mentioned it…"

"We can always call him in the morning," Barn interrupted reasonably.

Jenny returned with their drinks before Arnie could reply to his partner's comment.

"Are you folks ready to order?" she asked cheerily. "We have a special tonight…seafood chowder."

Pleasantly reciting the memorized description of the meal, she informed her hungry guests, "It's in a New England style broth with clams, lobster, scallops and shrimp. It comes with a baked potato and salad, and it's just $12.99."

Barn, the only person at the table to look at his menu, pushed it to one side, and no one else even bothered to check out the culinary competition.

Before scuttling off to put in four orders for today's special, Jenny paused to light the candle at the center of their table. As the tiny flame flickered to life, tossing sparks of gold into the eyes of the diners cozily gathered around the table, Jenny flashed her toothpaste commercial smile again, and proudly announced, "There, that's better. I'll be right back with a basket of bread for you."

Watching the waitress' retreating back, Jack said, "Tell us about the people at the inn, son. Remember, we walked in at the end of it; we don't actually know too much about the beginning."

Arnie, golden specks of light now reflecting off of his tight, tawny curls, began the introductions.

"Gretchen Grissom, the lady from the tavern across the green, told Barn and I that George Parker, the guy who owns the inn, has a history of violence toward women… she said he beat his wife…"

"Yeah, but she never said anything about using an axe on her," Barn interpolated.

"No, I know that, Peanut," Arnie said, grinning as he saw both of the Fentnors break into smiles; his new nickname for his partner was a hit. "I doubt he did it; he's cold, but I can't see anyone hacking someone's head off, and then coming in to fix coffee."

"I want to get back to the girls for just a minute," Helene said. "I'd have to think the police will look pretty hard at Lizzie, just because they were traveling together."

Looking from Barn to Arnie, she said, "The fact that they were fighting twice the day before Gloria turned up dead, doesn't look too good for her, does it?"

With a slight shudder, she finished, "But I can't think of a woman doing that."

245

"Lizzie Borden took an axe…" Arnie began, the candlelight reflecting in his hazel eyes making them appear golden.

Helene responded, "Oh, I know it's been done, sweetheart. I just don't like to think about it. That seems more like something a man would do…Lizzie Borden excepted, of course."

Jenny returned to the table once more, and the party again fell silent as she set down a large wicker basket full to over-flowing with bread, rolls and butter.

Barn, waiting to respond to Helene's last comment, watched the scene outside gradually metamorphosing from late afternoon to early twilight. The last of the sun's rays were hitting the edges of the apple tree's amber leaves, painting them with fire, while the night's blue shadows crept over the lawn, swallowing it in slow gulps.

"Of course," Barn said, helping himself to a roll from the basket as soon as Jenny left. Watching her sashaying toward the kitchen again, he commented, "They could use her at Punky's."

"I take it their service hasn't improved since the night we ate there," Jack said, referring to a restaurant where the four of them had dined over a year ago—the poor service apparently being an omen of things to come. Pleasant company and good food aside, the long evening had played out as the opening scene to a multi-day pageant of family tragedy.

Barn shook his head, saying, "No, in fact, I think it's worse—but let's get back to business. I don't like Sydney Slating; he's here with his sister. She's nice, but he's a bastard. I can't honestly say that I caught more than a glimpse of him all day, but from what I saw yesterday, he's not normal...he went off at Gloria the other morning like she'd committed a crime by not coming to breakfast before."

"I think he's got an emotional problem," Arnie said, gingerly breaking a chunk of hot, crusty bread apart. "His sister said something about how he shouldn't let 'this thing' ruin his entire life."

"Umm...I remember that," Barn said, watching the steam rising from the bread his partner was buttering; it looked good, and he reached for a piece to keep the roll on his plate company.

"I wonder what it was...divorce, maybe?" he mused aloud, taking an accurate stab at information he was still not privy to.

"Didn't the guests get to talk to each other at all today?" Jack asked, wondering if they had been warned to remain apart.

"Not really," Barn answered. "This morning after Mr. Parker called Russ Johnson, he told everyone to go back up to their rooms. Sydney Slating was still out on his walk. Jane Slating took Lizzie upstairs because she was crying so hard, but I doubt any discussion took place."

Nodding his head slightly in his partner's direction, he said, "Arnie and I just sat in our room wondering what in hell was going on."

Barn paused for a moment, drinking in the peaceful twilight scene outside the window. "From what I can tell, after everyone talked to Russ Johnson, they went right up to their rooms again. When Russ and I found the body, and there was all that commotion going on, everyone came back down, but by the time Kittery got here, everyone was back up in their own rooms again...we never talked as a group."

It was true; there had been no fraternizing among the guests. It seemed logical to expect that morbid curiosity would drag them away from the rooms they had returned to after their first and second rounds of questioning, but that had not been the case. No one emerged until late in the afternoon; even Parker had ducked out of sight. It was as though the inn had been programmed for silence.

Helping himself to the bread before Barn and Arnie finished it off by themselves, Jack said, "If Barn's guess about a divorce is right, this Slating man could just be very bitter...it wouldn't be the first time something like that happened. Being insufferably rude to people you aren't likely to see again is a far cry from being able to hoist an axe and whack their heads off."

Helene held her hand up, and counted off on her fingers, "George Parker, Lizzie Tidman, Sydney Slating, Jane Slating...four, so far. Is there anyone else at the inn?"

"No, just us," Arnie answered.

"Who's this Gretchen somebody that Arnie first mentioned?" Jack asked, buttering still-warm bread. "I don't remember where she figures in."

Arnie was chewing, so Barn fielded the inquiry. "She runs the tavern across the green...Arnie said that. She's got nothing to do with the inn, other than that she hates Parker; his wife was her friend."

"All right, so that leaves us with three, no four people, who, maybe, could have done it..." Helene began.

Swallowing, Arnie responded, "No, go back to three. I think we can rule Jane Slating out. I can't imagine what would tie her to Gloria Baines."

"Maybe she wanted to date Lizzie" Barn suggested, to the astonishment of his three tablemates.

Arnie locked eyes with his partner for a second, and then asked, "Do you think there's something...was something... with Lizzie and Gloria?"

Barn chewed his roll thoughtfully, and then answered, "I really don't know...probably not, not sexual, anyway." Taking a sip of water, he added, "Still, there's something funny there. I can feel it, but I just can't put my finger on it."

"Can you explain it at all?" Jack asked, his eyes intently studying Barn.

"I'm not sure," Barn confessed. "It's just a strange situation, I think. Gloria insulted Lizzie in the car, but then, just before they started to quarrel in the antiques shop, she offered to buy her a string of pearls that cost well over $100..."

So far, Helene had avoided the extra carbohydrates, but the bread was calling her name. Reaching for a slice, she said, "But it goes back to what I said a minute ago...they had two fights yesterday, and today Gloria's dead. It just doesn't look good."

Jack queried, "But don't girlfriends do things like that... buy gifts to make peace?"

"Maybe, but this seemed different...it was almost like she was trying to appease her somehow," Barn said.

"But why would Lizzie need to be appeased?" Helene wondered, not expecting to be enlightened.

"No idea," Barn said.

The tinny strains of 'It's a Small World' sounding from around Arnie's waist ended any chance for further debate.

Barn rolled his dark eyes, and grumbled, "Damned cellular instrument of torture. Arnie's always changing the ring, but this is the worst." Coming from someone who stood a cool 60" tall, his feeling was understandable.

"Hello," Arnie said, poking one finger into his ear to block out his partner's voice.

"Arnie?"

"Uh, uh…who's this?" Arnie's eyes reflected the puzzled sound of his voice.

"Lizzie Tidman."

"Lizzie?" he repeated incredulously.

His tablemates looked equally puzzled as he continued to speak into the phone. "How did you get this number?"

"The guest registry…I remembered Mr. Parker asked us for a phone number when we checked in, so I thought he probably did the same thing with you—I hoped it was for a cell phone."

"Oh, I'd forgotten about that," Arnie said. "I did give him this number. Where are you?"

"I'm in the parking lot…I followed you guys. Can I come in? I really need to talk."

Arnie looked up at his tablemates. Six curious eyes silently asked for an explanation.

He covered the mouthpiece and said, "It's Lizzie...she followed us here. Anyone mind if she comes in?"

"You mean she literally followed us...she's in the parking lot or something?" Barn asked.

"Parking lot," Arnie confirmed. "She says she's gotta talk to us. I don't know what it's about."

As usual, Helene wasted no time making her point. "It's gotta be good, if she's sneaking around like Spies R Us. Tell her to get her ass in here."

"Come on in, Lizzie" Arnie said, smiling at the 'Spies R Us' comment. "You'll see us right away. It's a small place, and we're right in front of the window."

At her end of the line, the young blond looked around the parking lot. She was glad no one else was in sight; she would have hated to have other people see her shaking so badly.

"I'll be right in" she said, and Arnie could hear the tremor in her voice.

Chapter 22

Lizzie Tidman walked into the small restaurant, and spoke briefly to the hostess. "I'm joining the party of four by the window," she said.

The hostess picked up a menu, and walked with her to the table, where she pulled a chair over for the young woman, placing it between Barn and Helene.

"Jenny'll be right back to take your order," she said, before walking back to her station right inside the door.

Without waiting for a formal introduction, since she was sure one had been made between the time Arnie disconnected and the time she walked through the door, Lizzie said, "I'm just gonna say this right out, because there's no easy way to lead into it. Glo didn't work in a bank, at least not anymore. She was a paralegal…"

Barn was the first to interrupt. "I don't understand. Why did she say she worked in a bank?"

Before Lizzie could answer his question, he noticed Super Waitress returning, and said, "Hold it a second...here comes the waitress; just order the special and whatever you want to drink."

Lizzie did as she was told, and, after assuring the others that she would have their orders kept warm until the newest order was ready, Jenny went back to the kitchen, pleased that the special of the day was such a big hit.

Tucking a long lock of golden hair behind one ear, Helene said, "She's quick, so let's just talk about nothing much until she comes back with Lizzie's soda and place setting."

As the others nodded their agreement, Lizzie said, "All right," and looked out the window. "It must be a pretty view in the daytime," she said. "It's getting too dark now to really see much of it, except what we can see from the light inside here."

Glancing from Jack to Helene, seated at opposite ends of the table, she asked, "Are y'all just friends, or what? We haven't met before...are you at the inn now, too?"

"I'm sorry," Arnie said. "You didn't give me time to introduce my parents...Jack and Helene."

"Nice to meet you. I'm Lizzie Tidman, but I guess you know that." She smiled self-consciously, before asking, "Are you here for the wedding...or did they postpone it?"

Looking at the young men quickly, she inquired, "You haven't, have you? There's no reason to."

"No, we're still gonna do it," Arnie said. "We talked about whether or not we should...it's really not the kind of thing you want to remember every year when you have an anniversary, but realistically, Barn's work schedule is pretty hectic, and I'm at school...it wasn't easy clearing this time...so we decided to go ahead. We didn't know when we could do it again."

Jenny returned with Lizzie's soda and place setting, and everyone fell silent for the minute it took her to deposit them on the table. With a huge smile, she assured them, "The last order will be up soon, and I'll bring everything out at once."

"Thank you," Helene answered for the group.

"Go ahead, Lizzie," Arnie prompted once Jenny had disappeared again.

The young receptionist picked up her story. "Well" she said, "Glo used to work in a bank, in the mortgage closing department over at First Mutual of Bryant..."

"As a paralegal?" Helene asked. Prepared to be suspicious of the girl now beside her, she found herself liking her straight off instead.

"Yes, that's right," Lizzie said, gazing into Helene's eyes—it was easier to talk to another woman. "She was a paralegal there, and she just switched jobs a few months ago…maybe eight months ago."

"I don't understand why she lied about where she worked, Lizzie," Arnie said.

Lizzie answered, shaking her head in disbelief of the words she herself was about to relate.

"Because she's 100% not the person I thought she was when I met her at the salon…."

"How long ago was that?" Arnie asked, giving the breadbasket a gentle shove in the new diner's direction.

"Not quite two years, I guess," Lizzie answered, automatically reaching for the bread. "I wish she'd taken her damned hair someplace else," she said.

Her next words were even more surprising. "She was a conniving, manipulative little bitch…"

"So why are you traveling with her…unless you've just made this personality assessment recently?" Barn interpolated.

Lizzie's dark green eyes flashed with anger. "No, she's here…or she was here…because she forced her way into my trip. I'll explain the minutiae in a second, but she figured she could impress her boss…maybe get a big raise…if she could get Gretchen Grissom to sell the tavern…"

Words previously dismissed as small talk, now rang in Arnie's ears with new meaning.

Looking directly at his partner, he interrupted Lizzie by saying, "Barn, do your remember Gretchen making a comment that first night about someone taking a notion to build up here?"

"Yeah," Barn quickly answered. "She said something about there being so much empty space no one needed to be asked to leave their property…something like that. I didn't attach any meaning to it…"

"I didn't either, but this has to be what she was talking about."

Looking at the young woman seated beside his partner, he asked, "Have they been after her for a long time, Lizzie… do you know?"

Buttering her bread as though her life depended on it, she said, "I don't really know, but probably yes. Glo told me her firm only had until the end of the month to wrap it up. I guess the developer's gonna go someplace else then; they must have been working on this for a fairly long time."

257

"Gretchen can't have more than six acres there. Is George Parker involved too?" Arnie asked intuitively.

"Yes...I definitely know that much. Parker is already on board to sell his property too. He's got over 20 acres, but everything is hanging on whether or not Gretchen will sell, because they'll need extra land for expansion later on."

"I think you're missing something," Barn said, watching as the bread was treated to a second layer of butter.

"What?" Lizzie asked, dropping the bread, buttered side down onto the tablecloth. She quickly scooped it up and dropped it onto her bread plate where it would remain untouched throughout the rest of her story.

"It's big and grassy, and sits right between Boardwalk and Park Place."

"The green?" Lizzie said.

"Yeah...the green, or am I the one missing something?" Barn asked.

"It's you," the nervous blond answered. "George Parker owns the green."

"Interesting" Jack said, "but I want to ask you something before you go on, Lizzie, if you don't mind."

"Sure, Jack...what?"

"Why would a paralegal be sent up here to work on a huge real estate deal? Isn't that a bit out of their normal realm of responsibilities?"

"Yes, but everyone else in the firm failed, apparently, so she approached her boss like a real estate superhero or something, and said she could do it because she had some information…wait a minute, I'm getting ahead of myself. Let me start with why I was planning to come up here in the first place."

Jenny arrived with the tray at that point, so conversation ended again while the meals were being laid out.

"Do you need anything else right now?" Jenny asked pleasantly.

"No, we're all set," everyone answered, displaying spontaneous choral speaking skills that were remarkably good.

The waitress left them to enjoy their meals, and the conversation resumed.

"Go on, Lizzie, you were about to tell us why you planned to come to Vermont," Helene prompted.

Lizzie took a sip of her soda. "I should've ordered something stronger," she said, before picking up the story again. "My mother's name used to be Millie Cushman, and she grew up here. By the time I was born, she had moved to Maryland…"

"I remember you mentioning that at breakfast yesterday," Barn said, turning his head to look at the girl seated beside him.

The fifth member of the dining party inclined her head slightly, and then continued speaking. "The reason for that was because she'd had an affair with a married man— she didn't know he was married at the time. She wasn't married, but that didn't make her any less pregnant…"

Arnie and Barn exchanged knowing glances across the table, before Barn factitiously said, "We should start a support group."

"Watch yourself, mister," Helene said.

Barn grinned at her. "Sorry, I forgot who you were for a second."

Helene laughed, unable to resist Barn's good humor. "Forgive us, Lizzie," she said. "We didn't mean to interrupt, it's just that both of the boys were in a similar situation. Jack and I were teenagers when Arnie was born, and Barn's parents had to get married. You have a sympathetic audience, Lizzie…go on."

Seeming somewhat relieved, Lizzie Tidman again resumed her story. "If you've been in my mother's position…or your mother was in that same boat…you can understand something of how Mom felt; she was horribly embarrassed."

"Did she tell him?" Helene asked.

"Yes…that's when she learned he was married."

"No idea at all before then?" Jack asked, wondering how the man had managed to keep his marital status a complete secret.

Lizzie shrugged her shapely shoulders. "I honestly don't know. Mom's told me that the relationship barely lasted four months, so it's possible that she just hadn't begun to suspect anything yet."

"Didn't she have any family in Vermont to turn to, dear?" Helene asked.

"No, her parents were divorced, and she wasn't close to either of them; this will sound horrible, but I honestly don't know if they're still living," the young woman admitted.

"Anyway" she continued, "Mom ended up going to Maryland to live with her aunt, Sadie Tidman, who was my grandmother's sister…"

"Did her parents know where she went, or didn't it matter?" Helene queried, spooning up her first taste of seafood chowder.

"I doubt that it mattered," Lizzie answered. "Mom told both of them that she was pregnant, but neither one of them even cared enough to yell at her…and, of course, she'd told my father, but he couldn't do anything about it, so she just left."

"Did he have any idea where she went?" Barn asked.

"No, she didn't tell him," she said, taking a long sip of her root beer. "For all he knows" she added, "Mom could've had an abortion or even died herself...she never contacted him about child support."

"Was your aunt originally from Maryland, or did she move down from Vermont, too?" queried Helene.

Lizzie answered, "Aunt Sadie lived in Vermont until about the time Mom got out of high school, and then she moved to Maryland. I guess she'd been living there for three or four years when Mom got pregnant. Anyway, when Mom called her and told her about everything, Aunt Sadie said she should come right down, and live with her. Mom made the move, and before I was born, she changed her name from Millie Cushman to Millie Tidman."

"You've lived with her all these years?" Jack asked.

"Yes," Lizzie acknowledged. "We lived with her right up until the end of last summer, when she died. She was, like, 93 or something. She left a lot of bills...her medical insurance was lousy. Mom's stuck with them now, unless she wants to see the house attached...and probably lost."

Drawing a deep, quavering breath, Lizzie said, "This is how I ended up owing Gloria Baines a favor, and having her company on this trip. I went to her because her job pays big time, and I asked her if she could help. She said she needed to think about it overnight, which seemed reasonable, because it's a big sum of money I'm talking about."

"But she came to you the next day with more than a 'yes' or 'no' answer," Jack stated. No stranger to the world of wheeling and dealing, thanks to his deceased banker father, the well-mannered oral surgeon could already smell the rat crawling out of the woodpile.

"A lot more," Lizzie said. "She knew about my mother's affair. I told her about it one night when we went out for drinks after work. I should have kept my mouth shut, but I had known her for enough time that I thought I could trust her…and that's the same time I told her I was going to Vermont in October to look my father up."

She paused to wipe her eyes, which had filled with frustrated tears. "I didn't want to meet him. I don't want anything from him…I just wanted to see what he looked like. I know that sounds crazy, but I just wanted to see him."

The pretty blond brushed away a few more angry tears, and continued speaking. "She said she'd give my mother the money outright, not a loan, if I'd agree to let her come along on this trip…"

"Too small a payback for a very big favor," Jack said knowingly.

Lizzie nodded her blond mane. "I thought so too" she said, "and I asked her what else I had to do. She told me as much as I've told you about the real estate deal, and then said she wanted to use my story...sort of...to persuade Gretchen to sell the property to her."

"Hold it," Jack said. "Are you saying she was going to present herself as Whit's daughter?"

Lizzie had to smile at the instinctive intuitiveness of Arnie's father.

"Bingo," she said.

"Holy shit," Barn said. "That puts a new light on everything, doesn't it?"

A hundred light bulbs coming on in his head at once, Arnie said, "It was gonna happen last night...that's why you suddenly decided to get all of us out of there."

Her eyes swimming with tears, a trembling Lizzie admitted, "Yes, but I didn't want to. God, I hated doing it; Gretchen's such a nice lady..."

Jack interrupted, "Lizzie, this is extortion. Why didn't you just go to the police? Legally, you can be considered an accomplice, regardless of whether or not you wanted to do it."

He studied the young woman's suddenly horrified face, and saw the answer. A mild-mannered, slightly timid girl, she had been cowed by a stronger personality and failed to consider that there could be repercussions far worse than having her mother financially and personally embarrassed.

"Oh…God, no, no, I really had nothing to do with her plan," she urgently stressed, her shaking hands clasping tightly together on the edge of the table. "I didn't think of the police." Calling on the Almighty again, she said miserably, "God, I never thought…"

Placing one hand comfortingly over Lizzie's clenched fists, Barn said, "Never mind that for now, Lizzie; how was her masquerade going to get Gretchen to sell the tavern? Do you have any idea what else she was planning to tell her?" Barn asked.

Wretchedly, Lizzie said, "I know it all." Unclenching her fists and taking up her butter knife, just to have something to twist around in her trembling fingers, she continued, "Her story was gonna be that she lived farther up north, and got wind of a huge real estate deal…she wasn't gonna say how…she didn't need to. All she needed to do was threaten to make the story public, unless Gretchen sold her the tavern for its actual fair market value."

"I don't think 'bitch' is a good enough word…that's diabolical." Helene said. "How could she be sure the woman would believe her? My own first thought would have been that she was lying."

"No offense intended here, Helene, but you aren't in the situation," Lizzie whispered. "Listening to something you're just hearing about, you know what to do…it's not always that clear when you're the one living through it—and I guess my stupidity in not calling the police proves that. Besides, Glo could be very persuasive, and the story had the ring of truth to it just because it was so blatantly rotten."

Lizzie Tidman had not wanted this to happen, Jack and the others could clearly see that; they also saw that the moment she confided a family secret to a manipulative woman she believed to be her friend, she had unwittingly set herself up. It was impossible to gauge her innermost emotions, but her feelings of shame and remorse were clearly painted on her young face.

Jack disliked having to ask the next question. Ordinarily he was not a man who pried into the personal lives of others, but her answer might also be the answer to who committed the crime.

"Lizzie" he began, "this has nothing to do with what you should or shouldn't have done—it's more important than that. Are you Whit Grissom's daughter?"

Lizzie drew a deep breath, and let it out with her answer.

"No, I'm Mitch Kittery's daughter."

Four astonished voices said, "Jesus Christ!"

"I know…amazing, isn't it? I don't remember what I even said when he was questioning me; I probably made myself look guilty. It was just that when I recognized him from a picture Mom gave me, the picture I brought with me, I got so upset and nervous I couldn't even look at him. I had no idea what he did for a living. I was just gonna look his name up in the book, and go by his place…see if I could catch a glimpse of him."

"Don't worry about that…we'll go with you to see him, and you can tell him the whole story."

Remembering something else that he had dismissed earlier, Arnie said, "Were the two of you talking about this in the car before we left for those shops yesterday morning? We saw both of you gesturing with your hands while you were talking, but a lot of people do that…"

"Yes, we were," Lizzie answered. "I tried to talk her out of it…she told me she was planning to talk to Gretchen that night, and I was supposed to get you to go to the movies. We were both pretty hot, but we managed to put a lid on it…just barely…before you guys heard what we were saying."

"But that's why she got snotty with you right afterwards, isn't it?" Barn asked.

"Yes," Lizzie confirmed.

For the benefit of Jack and Helene, she explained further, "I'd tried to talk her out of it, and she got mad. When the guys got back in the car and we were gonna head for the shops, she made a nasty comment about me being stupid for passing an antiques place the day before…but she thought better of it later, and tried to make up by buying me a present. I refused, and we ended up having more words in the store."

"I guess that explains all the pictures," Barn said suddenly. Like Arnie, he was now attaching significance to things that had seemed banal yesterday.

Arnie was quick to admit, "I hadn't even thought of them. She took dozens and dozens of pictures all along the road on the way back to the inn."

Explaining it further to Jack and Helene, Barn responded, "Yeah, and there we stood like two idiots, watching while she took pictures of the road that provides ingress and egress to the biggest parcel of land in the area…assuming Gretchen would sell out. Obviously, her boss will have a surveyor take more later; in fact, they may already have some, but why not take a bunch herself, as long as we were right there?"

The small party was silent for a few seconds, everyone digesting the content of their conversation.

Finally Barn said, "It looks like Gloria talked to Gretchen last night, and lost her head for her troubles…talk about underestimating the possibilities."

Chapter 23

"Please tell me you had nothing to do with this, Syd," Jane Slating said. She was seated on the edge of her bed, still in the clothes she had worn all day. Her small hands, clenched into fists, were in her lap.

Her brother, standing by the room's only window, turned around to face her. Arrogantly, he sneered, "Why would I waste my time on a tramp like her, Jane?"

The woman rose, and walked over to where her older brother stood.

"Sydney!" she exclaimed.

Studying the now hate filled face of a man who had once been so kind, she softened her tone, and whispered, "Since your divorce, I've watched you change from a sweet, gentle man into a woman-hating, neurotic fool…"

"You don't know what I went through…." Sydney began, his voice irate.

His sister cut him off, but her voice was still reasonable. "No, I don't know exactly what you went through, but I know as much as everyone else in Burnham knows. Your ex-wife cheated on you with every man willing to drop his fly."

Outraged, Sydney shouted, "Shut up, Jane. You don't know what you're talking about. She made a fool of me…"

"She didn't make a fool of you…you're the one making a fool of you," Jane shot back, her voice beginning to show the strain of barely repressed anger.

Their late parents had taught them to keep their chins up; the whole world was not required to feel sorry for them because they did not grab life's gold ring. No pride could be taken in hating the many, when it had only been the one who had hurt you. Sydney no longer seemed to understand that.

"I'm asking you straight out, Sydney," Jane said, keeping the pressure up. "Did you have anything to do with this?"

"You bitch!" Sydney exploded. "How can you ask me that? What reason would I have to kill that little tramp?"

Jane forced the sharp retort she had in mind back down her throat; there was a time when her brother would never have spoken to her—or to any woman—with such disrespect.

As calmly as she could, she queried, "What reason did you have to talk to her the way you did at breakfast, Syd?"

"Because she's clearly a tramp...or she was a tramp...and the blond's probably just like her," he said flatly. As he saw it, he was stating an undeniable fact.

His sister shook her head slowly from side to side; when she spoke, her voice was eerily similar to their long deceased mother's. "I don't know you now, Syd."

"Bullshit you don't know me," Sydney Slating fired back. "I'm the same man I always was, just not so gullible. Just because I can see now that women are out for what they can get..."

Jane could not bear to listen to the nonsense her brother was spewing off any longer. She cut him off sharply, saying, "I heard someone in the hall last night. I'm a fairly light sleeper, but not so light that you couldn't have gotten out of the room without me hearing you if you really put your mind to it. Were you out there, Syd? Did you stick that note under those girls' door?"

"No!" Sydney Slating barked, averting his gaze from his sister's.

"I wish I could believe you," Jane answered.

> <

The fuzzy teeth of sleep were already beginning to nibble at the edges of Arnie's consciousness when Barn came out of the bathroom, towel wrapped around his waist, torso naked.

Barn, equally drained by the day, but in no mood for sleep, ditched the towel, and crawled into bed.

Cuddling against Arnie, he poked his tongue seductively into his audio portal, sending sizzling shivers down the neck of the lucky ear's owner. "Wake up, babe," he whispered. "Let's play suspended science teacher and wounded recording engineer."

A smile briefly flitted over Arnie's lips, but it was quickly devoured by a cavernous yawn. He rubbed Barn's back, as the other man nestled in his arms, but after several minutes, it was apparent to him that a backrub was the best he could do.

It was a classic case of a willing spirit being held back by weak flesh. With embarrassment he admitted, "Peanut, I'm whipped…I can't. Let's sleep for a couple hours." Feeling like the new poster boy for ED, he offered lamely, "Sorry."

After another yawn he said, "I'll make it up to you tomorrow night…I promise."

"Yippee," Barn said.

Arnie muttered, "Be reasonable, Peanut. It's been a brutal day…"

Succumbing for a moment to uncharacteristic selfishness, Barn pouted, "Does it have to be a brutal night, too?"

"I'm not your personal joy stick," Arnie snapped, and then started to laugh, despite himself.

"Actually, you are" Barn was quick to respond. "It's not my fault your stick went on sabbatical in your hour of need."

With no comeback at the ready, Arnie jumped headlong into immaturity by rolling over, and turning his back on his tiny tormentor.

Following his partner across the surface of the uncomfortable mattress, Barn rested his cheek against Arnie's bony back, before saying, "Stop calling me 'Peanut'."

Still hoping to salvage the wonderfully sleepy feeling that he was ready to embrace seconds ago, Arnie answered, "I'm worn out, cut me some slack…and I'm referring to your size, not Junior's."

"Yeah, right," Barn grumbled, already deciding that, if he was not going to be satisfied, his partner was not going to sleep.

A few thoughts had been stirring around in his head since they left The Orange Acorn, and now was as good a time as any—maybe better—to discuss them.

He sat up before giving Arnie's right shoulder blade a jab sharp enough to make him roll over again.

Opening his eyes to a sight more imagined than seen, Arnie could tell that his partner was sitting cross-legged beside him on the bed, and had turned to face him.

He muttered, "Why won't you leave me for someone else...anyone?"

Barn grinned. "I need to ask you a question," he said.

"I already said no, Barnaby" Arnie said, stressing his partner's name. "Settle back down, and go to sleep."

"That's not the question, Arnold," Barn answered.

Sighing resignedly, Arnie said, "All right...ask your question, and then let me sleep."

Barn came quickly to the point.

"Can you really see Gretchen swinging an axe like a baseball bat, and whacking off Gloria's head?" he asked.

Struck by a sudden fit of gallows humor, he commented, "It must've looked more like a pop-fly than a homerun."

Arnie, feeling his stomach churn at the thought of the old woman feeling the impact traveling up her arms to her shoulders, neck and back as the sharp, heavy blade of the axe struck Gloria's slender neck, said, "Barn, don't be disgusting."

"'Don't be disgusting'? Jesus, Arnie, how do you think it looked on the ground...pleasant? I saw it. It was not pleasant at all. I have to agree with what Mrs. Fentnor said before Lizzie got to the restaurant. I can't make myself think that a woman did this. Lizzie Borden aside, I just don't see it happening."

Against his own will, Arnie was now wide-awake. In the sliver of moonlight slicing the room, he could see the earnestness on his partner's face and the fire in his dark eyes.

Against his will, he was pulled into the hypothesis he had not wanted to hear tonight. "Who then, Sherlock?" he asked.

"Why not Whit?" Barn said simply.

"He doesn't own the property," Arnie answered.

"Come on, Arnie, make the leap, it's not a big one," Barn urged, leaning forward now so that his forearms were resting on his bare knees.

"Picture it. You're Gretchen, and Gloria's just confronted you, and told you she's Whit's illegitimate daughter. She

275

says she'll keep her mouth shut, but only if you all but give her the property you've been fighting to hang onto. What are you gonna do?"

"Go back and kick Whit in the balls," Arnie said automatically.

Barn responded, "Good choice...who knows, maybe she's done that, but what I was thinking was that more than likely, she'd rip the old bastard another asshole, and then tell him he made this mess, he can fix it. I doubt she meant for him to kill the girl...maybe buy her off somehow."

"So you're saying you think Whit did it?" Arnie asked, propping himself up on one elbow.

"It makes sense," Barn said urgently. "Think about it. He'd have every bit as much to lose...it's his only home too, and she waits on him hand and foot. Why not?"

"What about the bypass?"

"Earth to Arnie," Barn mocked, "You don't think he could take one swing? Come on, he'd be able to do that. It's been since last summer, babe. He's recovered...it's not a physical impossibility."

"I guess not, but my money's still on her," Arnie said, not ready to give up. For no particular reason he mused, "I wonder if they've found the axe yet."

"It's probably in the bottom of an old outhouse somewhere...that's long been a theory for how Lizzie Borden disposed of her weapon....but why is your money still on Gretchen?"

Arnie responded, "According to Parker, Russ Johnson was at the tavern this morning fixing the shed on the door. Gretchen claimed she'd heard something, probably a raccoon, out there last night. That had to be a cover story—she'd been out there herself."

Barn shook his head vigorously. "No...you've got your days mixed up. Sunday night was when she heard the noise...the confrontation didn't take place until Monday night, so why would she be getting an axe on Sunday?"

"Shit, that's right," Arnie acknowledged.

"Besides" Barn continued reasonably, "there was something by the shed. I saw it when we were leaving the tavern that first night..."

"I didn't see anything," Arnie interpolated.

"Well, I did," Barn answered. "It was when you were having some cold feet about getting married, and we were joking around a little bit...remember that?"

"Yes, I do."

"Well, when you were laughing, I happened to glance around the green and back toward the tavern. There was something…an animal of some kind…by the side of the shed. I didn't think much of it at the time, but if it went into the shed later on, Gretchen could've heard it."

"An animal…really?"

"Yeah…it seemed to be sitting up kind of, so it probably was a raccoon."

"Shit…maybe he did it," Arnie said.

Deliberately being obtuse to annoy his partner, Barn asked, "The raccoon?"

"No, you little pain in my ass…Whit."

"So, the great science master thinks the little knob turner is right about something?"

"You could be…you've raised a valid point."

"Good…I won," Barn gloated. "Now can we make love?"

Arnie laughed, teasing, "You'd be great in a war, Barn. 'OK troops, we won that battle. You know what it's time for now'!"

Giggling as he stretched out on the bed, Barn said, "Man the torpedoes," and snuggled back into Arnie's arms.

"No...no torpedoes yet" Arnie said, his voice suddenly dismal. Seeing all the neatly sewn together pieces beginning to unravel, he asked, "What about the note?"

"Shit," Barn said. "How'd I forget that?"

Climbing out of the warm, albeit lumpy, bed and into the chill of the drafty room, Barn began to pace—if it did not help him to think, at least it would get his blood moving.

"At least put your underwear on," Arnie encouraged. "It's not like I'm seeing much of the view...not that I'd object...but you'll freeze your dick off."

Ignoring the comments from his life partner and bed companion, Barn paced resolutely up and down the length of the cold, dark room, his mind tortured by an 'almost memory' that danced just outside the boundaries of his consciousness.

Like a bell sounding in a tomb, the exact memory, when it finally showed itself, was so startling that the bedroom's silent walker gasped in surprise; a satisfied grin appeared on his face, as he announced, "The note's not all we forgot about."

Chapter 24

Wednesday was the day Marge Kittery drove into town to do her grocery shopping. Her husband almost always worked in his office at home that day, so he was around to carry in the bulk of the order.

Marge and Mitch Kittery had a good marriage, despite his short-lived fling many years ago; for some reason, when Marge opened her eyes this morning, she had been struck with an almost violent recollection of the night her husband confessed his affair.

When he had confessed his infidelity, her husband also told her that his paramour had become pregnant; to their mutual surprise, the woman had moved away, and left no forwarding address.

Although Mitch had never heard from her again, Marge had known in her heart that one day she would open the door to find her husband's eyes peering back at her from another face.

When the bell rang as she was standing in the wide front hallway of their farmhouse pulling her coat on, Marge instinctively knew the day was here.

An uneasy feeling crawled down into her stomach, and settled there like a dragon waiting to breathe fire on an unsuspecting medieval village.

She hung her coat back up, and headed toward the sound of the bell.

The young people on the other side of the Kittery's broad, weathered front door had made the 30-minute drive up from Maple Grove Junction, talking all the way about the conversation two of them had in their bed the previous night and the conversation they would be having once they reached their destination this morning.

"Can I help you?" Marge asked tentatively.

Her eyes took in the sight of two young men flanking a slender blond woman, who appeared to be about 23 years old.

The dragon in her stomach swished its horned tail; not only was the woman on her doorstep the right age, she had the right eyes—Mitch's. Marge had never known anyone with eyes quite the same color as his. They were an iridescent shade of green that was nearly as deep and lustrous as emeralds.

"Yes," the man with blond hair answered. "We're looking for Sergeant Kittery…are we at the right house?"

"You are," Marge answered, adding, "I'm his wife. Is this police business?" 'God, let it be police business', she prayed, even though she already knew it was not.

The man who had spoken before answered her question. "Yes, but not entirely, ma'am. Sergeant Kittery interviewed the three of us yesterday about the murder in Maple Grove Junction."

As he spoke, Arnie could see the look in Marge's eyes, and it was not merely inquisitive—it was fearful.

Briefly, he wondered what she was afraid of, but he had no time to ponder the question—if he had, he might have remembered Mitch Kittery's bottle green eyes, and known that the woman in the doorway saw those same eyes looking back at her now. As it was, Marge Kittery quickly said, "Come in."

Motioning to the first door on their right, Marge instructed, "Go ahead in there and sit down…I'll get my husband."

She closed the door behind the young people, and scurried back up the hall toward the den, like a nervous Parisian mouse seeking a wheel of unguarded Brie.

"Mitch, there're some people to see you," she called out to her husband, working in the den.

The Kittery's den, like their kitchen, faced east, allowing the morning sun to pour in freely, unless the mini blinds were at least partially closed; this morning, with his mind on the Baines' murder, Mitch failed to make the adjustment. Looking up at the sound of his wife's voice, he found himself squinting in the direct sunlight.

"One of these days, I've gotta turn this damned desk around," he muttered, for the umpteenth time. Rising from his chair, he followed the sound of Marge's voice out into the hallway of their 100-year-old farmhouse.

Marge, a robust looking woman, whose tangle of curly hair had skipped gray and gone straight into white, was hustling toward him, her brown eyes overflowing with alarmed anticipation.

"They said it's about the murder yesterday down in the Grove," she whispered to him. "I've put them in the sitting room."

"All right, honey," Mitch answered, wondering why his wife looked so panicky, and why she was whispering about their early morning visitors.

"Did they say what they wanted?" he asked, as they walked back toward the den together.

"No…only that you interviewed them yesterday…"

Ever the detective, Mitch queried, "How many of them?" He had interviewed several people yesterday…he hoped he would not find the sour-faced Sydney Slating sitting in his favorite chair and the equally unpleasant George Parker on the sofa.

"Three," Marge answered, as they drew near the door. "Young people, a girl and two fellas," she clarified, nodding her head toward the dark wood of the sitting room's battered old door. She wanted to add that the woman had green eyes, but kept the thought to herself, praying that she was mistaken.

"OK," Mitch said. "I know who they are—I don't think any of 'em's the killer," he smiled, giving his wife's arm a gentle squeeze. "Relax, honey," he said, opening the door, and stepping aside so his wife could enter before him.

"Mitch is right here," Marge said, moving quickly into the room.

As Mitch stepped up beside her, they looked like a modern-day American Gothic. The man, dressed casually in charcoal slacks and a thick blue sweater, looked pleasantly surprised to see his guests; the woman, despite being dressed in well-worn jeans and an over-sized gray flannel shirt, seemed uncomfortable.

Barn and Arnie stood up, each stepping forward to shake the beefy hand of Mitch Kittery.

"Morning, boys," the owner of the large hand said.

Looking down at Lizzie, still seated on the sofa, hands neatly folded in her lap, Kittery said, "Good morning, Lizzie." He had felt yesterday that the girl had more to tell him; her presence here this morning confirmed it.

"Hi," Lizzie said softly, as her companions resumed their seats, one on each side of her on the green plaid divan.

"What can I do for you kids this morning?" the sergeant asked, still on his feet, but heading for his chair.

Arnie spoke. "We have some news for you. Please understand Lizzie didn't intend for it to come out this way; she didn't intend for you to know at all."

Marge Kittery took a chair. She could almost hear the words before they were spoken. A part of her used to wonder what she would ever do if, someday, the product of her husband's brief affair appeared at their door.

The dragon in her stomach was snorting fire; she knew she was about to find out.

"Know what?" Mitch asked, still in the dark.

Lizzie found her voice, small and shaky as it was. "I'm Millie Cushman's daughter...and yours," she said simply.

To Marge's relief, the visibly nervous young woman on her sofa appeared to want nothing at all—except to be anywhere else; with six simple, trembling words, tears were already filling her bottle green eyes.

Mitch dropped his heavyset frame into his sturdy, overstuffed chair; he had chosen his favorite well—the other chairs in the room looked as though they would have failed the test had he dropped his full weight onto them all at once.

"Oh my God," the stunned man gasped.

He regained his composure in the time it took him to speak the three words.

Almost at once, he was on his feet, pulling his newfound daughter up and into his strong arms. They clung tightly to one another, the instinctive familial bond holding them together like glue.

The sitting room's other three occupants watched father and daughter embrace, and each of them felt a swelling in their throats.

Even Marge, who seconds ago had been terrified, now bit back an unexpected sob at the sight of her husband holding his grown child in his arms, weeping for the time he had lost with his only progeny.

When the embrace finally ended, Mitch, in a voice choked with emotion, said, "Tell me everything, Lizzie. Why did you come here? What happened with Gloria Baines?"

Lizzie sat back down on the sofa again, and this time her father sat beside her.

Barn, standing up to allow the sergeant to have his seat, cocked a forefinger in his partner's direction. "Come on," he said. Arnie stood up, and followed his partner toward the door.

Just a step ahead of his curly-haired friend, Barn bent to touch Marge's arm as he reached her chair. "I think we should let 'em alone," he said. "Arnie and I can tell you everything she's gonna say."

><

"I'm afraid I don't even know your names," Marge said to the young men who followed her into the sun-filled kitchen. Her husband had not gotten as far as making introductions; the tawny haired man had come to the reason for their visit almost instantaneously.

The same man now handled introductions in the homey kitchen, "I'm Arnie Kotkin," he said. "This is my friend, Barnaby Moss," he informed their hostess, careful not to say the dreaded moniker 'Barn Moss'.

"I'm Marge Kittery," the woman explained needlessly, having already introduced herself at the front door. She headed toward the counter by the sink, where the coffeemaker reigned over the welcoming room.

Large, sunny and spotless, the kitchen was not modern; the appliances were dated, and cabinets were non-existent. Open shelving, fastidiously covered with white paper, lined one entire wall, and the couple's dry goods, undecorated dishes, and well-used pots and pans were on permanent display.

"Just let me fix us some fresh coffee," Marge said, "and then you can tell me what this is all about."

Minutes later, with the scent of freshly-brewing coffee filling the air, Barn began to tell the story Lizzie related last night at The Orange Acorn—a story which, implausible as it might seem at first blush, still carried the ring of truth.

> <

Telling her tale to her father as they sat side-by-side on the tired old sofa, Lizzie felt less afraid than she had in weeks.

Looking around the large room as she spoke, she learned something of her father's character. Seeing him in action yesterday, she already knew he was a hardworking man; today, seeing his home, she knew he enjoyed a simple lifestyle.

The room in which father and daughter sat was rectangular in shape. Paneled with what was once light pine, the room's lower half now wore wainscoting that had darkened over the years to the color of light rust.

Above the chair rail running around the room's perimeter, the walls were covered with a honey-hued oatmeal paper.

In the center of the long wall opposite the door, a huge, granite fireplace was framed by heavily curtained windows—the sitting room was a drafty place in winter—and topped with a rough-hewn mantle piece holding only a clock, a few bunches of dried flowers and a handful of bittersweet vines.

The world's kindest person would not have called the furniture a collection of valuable antiques; the old farmhouse's owners felt no compulsion to fill their home with the furnishings it had enjoyed in its early years. Instead, they treasured the old flea market finds they collected over the years, and took pleasure in their shared memories of finding just the right piece.

Mitch studied the face of the girl at his side, and wondered how he could have missed the resemblance yesterday. Except for her eyes, which were the same bottle green as his own, Lizzie Tidman was the image of her mother.

In her guileless, young visage, Mitch saw Millie's button nose, rosy cheeks and heart-shaped mouth. Her tiny face, like her mother's, was framed with fair hair that shone like wheat in the sun.

Still clutching her delicate hands in his own large, powerful ones as she finished speaking, Kittery stated, "So, once Gloria Baines found out about your past, she started concocting this scheme?"

Even knowing that the facts she related would have driven many people to put an axe to the grindstone and go out for batting practice, Mitch Kittery stood firm by the feeling he had gotten yesterday during their interview—Lizzie Tidman had nothing to do with the particularly cruel killing of her one-time friend.

"I guess so," Lizzie answered. "I can't help wondering if I hadn't told her about it, would she ever have shown me her true colors?"

Looking both embarrassed and saddened, the betrayed young woman said, "I really thought we were friends. I never trusted anyone else with the story; I feel like a complete fool...and Arnie's father said what Glo was doing was extortion, and I could've ended up as an accomplice."

"Well, the smart thing would've been to keep your mouth shut in the first place...but no one's smart everyday," Mitch answered.

Patting Lizzie's hand, he added, "There's no reason to worry about charges being filed against you, Liz; the situation came to murder, not to the obtainment of property, real or otherwise, through the application of undue pressure."

Sometimes Mitch reduced definitions to just a few words, other times, like now, he spieled off the entire thing.

"I still feel like an idiot," Lizzie said. "I know Arnie's father could've been entirely right if Gretchen had sold Gloria the tavern, and Glo hadn't been killed. I was so afraid, I never thought of going to the police…I'm usually not so stupid as this…" she said miserably, her voice trailing away.

Looking into eyes that matched his own, Mitch asked, "Was it just that you were trying to get your mother out of a jam that made you do this, or did Gloria Baines threaten you in some way?"

Once more, Lizzie looked deeply ashamed.

"No, she never threatened me, not specifically."

Taking a moment to decide how to explain her reasons for playing along with Gloria's scheme, she finally said, "After she told me her plan, and I saw how ruthless she was, I was afraid she'd blab Mom's secret everywhere…or even worse, tell Mom that I'd gone to her for money…that I just went along."

Again wiping tears of shame from her eyes, she said, "I feel almost like I blackmailed myself. Glo counted on me acting like a jellyfish, and I sure lived up to it…"

"Wait a minute, Lizzie," Kittery interrupted. "Do you mean your mother didn't know you'd gone to Gloria for money?"

The concept puzzled him, and he asked the obvious question, "If you'd gotten it, how were you going to explain it to her?"

"I told her I was trying to get a loan...I let her think I meant a personal loan from a bank," Lizzie answered.

Clearly embarrassed, she said again, "I can't believe I didn't think of going to the police...I don't know how I let myself get tied up in this."

Kittery nodded his head and said, "It's all right now, Lizzie," to his softly weeping daughter. "You'd seen what the woman was capable of, and you got scared...maybe too scared to think straight. Don't beat yourself up anymore."

He put his arm around her slim shoulders, and pulled her close to him. In a comforting way, he said, "Come on, girl. We'll figure this out..."

Lizzie interrupted, "You've gotta talk to Barn and Arnie about that. I think they have figured it out."

> <

"Unbelievable," Marge Kittery said over her coffee cup, before adding, "I suppose I shouldn't say that...being a cop's wife, I guess I've heard wilder tales."

The two men joining her for coffee that morning, had carefully recounted Lizzie Tidman's story, but her mind had not yet sorted everything out.

Putting her cup back into the saucer, with just the slightest clank, she said, "Clear up one point for me...I think I just didn't catch it all. How did the Baines woman get Lizzie to go along?"

Graciously accepting the blame for any misunderstanding, Barn answered, "I'm sorry, Mrs. Kittery, maybe I wasn't clear on that."

He took a sip of the dark liquid in his cup, picturing it eating the lining of his stomach, and said, "She's a pretty timid girl, actually; she was afraid of the consequence if she didn't. It was a bit like extortion, except the threats were never verbalized…"

Arnie interrupted, "In her defense, she tried like the devil to keep Gloria from having time alone with Gretchen, but that last night, it looks like she just succumbed to the inevitable."

Those were the words Mitch and Lizzie heard as they entered the kitchen.

"That's how it sounded to me, too," Mitch answered, directing his daughter to the empty chair at the head of the table, before going to retrieve a chair from beside the kitchen's plant-filled garden window.

Pulling his chair up to the table between his wife and Barn, Mitch said, "Lizzie tells me you boys think you've figured this thing out." He did not look like he quite believed it, and his voice lent credence to the doubtful expression in his eyes. He liked both young men, but life was not a TV crime show.

Barn answered before Arnie could even open his mouth.

"I doubt we know more than you do," he said. Accustomed to massaging the inflated egos of temperamental recording artists, Barn simply applied the same trick in explaining his theory to the veteran officer. "Last night, Arnie and I were thinking about the first night we were here—the first time we ever spoke to Gretchen Grissom over at the tavern."

Arnie added, "As far as we were concerned, the stuff she was telling us was just small talk, but looking back at it now, it's pretty interesting stuff."

With a nod toward Lizzie, Barn picked up his explanation again, saying, "Undoubtedly, you know all about the proposed swindle by now, Sergeant Kittery."

When he saw Lizzie's father incline his head, Barn said, "That first night, Gretchen made a vague reference to us about there being enough room to build up here, without people being put off their property, or words to that effect…"

Smiling tolerantly as he cocked a bushy brow upwards, Kittery interrupted. "Are you proposing now that the Grissom woman did this, Barn? Yesterday you were thinking of Lizzie…that's why you asked if a woman could've done it."

Lizzie, arms folded over her gray sweatshirt, grinned sheepishly, and acknowledged, "Thanks, I guess I deserved that." She had listened to the entire theory on the ride up here, but Barn never said that, at one time, he considered her a suspect.

Giving his former suspect an apologetic smile, Barn said, "Um, sorry…it was nothing personal." He added, "I just figured you did it because you came up here together—at least I did until after you told us everything last night…"

Arnie cut in again, saying, "It's not that your story doesn't make for a good motive, Lizzie, because it does. It's just that, after you told us everything, Barn could see that someone else had a better one…and I'm convinced that he's right."

Not yet convinced himself, Mitch asked, "Who had it, and what is it?"

Taking up the explanation of his theory again, Barn said, "It seems obvious now that Gretchen was talking about the way the developer, or, rather, the developer's attorney, had been harassing her about selling."

Pausing for a quick sip of coffee, and again thinking that Marge's brew was gnawing on his stomach lining, he said, "It had to amount to harassment, if everyone in the firm had been trying to coerce her into selling."

Scratching a denim-covered thigh, he said, "She talked a lot about her husband's affair that night. I doubt she's mad about it after all these years. I think it's just a good story to tell over the bar…"

"I've gotta talk to her today," Mitch interjected; he should have done it yesterday, but with all the interviews to be conducted at the inn, and the crime scene to be looked at again, interviewing the proprietress of the White Star Tavern about her broken shed door and possibly missing axe had been put on the 'things to do tomorrow' list.

Now that tomorrow was today, it seemed obvious to Kittery that this was going to be a very interesting 'talk'.

Intruding on the sergeant's private thoughts, Barn went on, "I think you'll find her to be quite entertaining. She'll tell you that the tavern is the only place she's ever lived, and that, aside from her husband...she'll call him the old bastard...that's all she got in the world..."

Mitch grinned, "OK, OK, Barn, I think you've made your point." He gave the young man a quick clap on the shoulder, adding, "I think I've got a pretty good idea of how it worked. Gloria Baines approached her, said she's Whit Grissom's illegitimate daughter, and wanted the property so she could make a fortune off it."

With a quick, slashing motion across his own neck, he said, "Next day, the old lady whacks her head clean off. Russ Johnson mentioned to me that the old lady chops firewood; that stuff's a lot harder than a skinny girl's neck."

"Um...no, actually, that's not quite what we think," Barn answered, a slightly lop-sided grin playing leap frog over his mouth by jumping away as soon as it touched his lips.

"It could've gone that way" he said, "but in all due respect, we think it went a different way."

As Kittery's eyebrows rose dangerously close to his hairline, Barn was struck with a sudden inspiration—a way to force the sergeant to see it in a different light. Looking at the older man's better half, he said, "Mrs. Kittery, do you mind if I use you as an example?"

Intuitively grasping the young man's plan, Marge answered, "Go ahead, Barnaby. I think it's a perfect analogy."

Barn looked back at Kittery, and said, "Suppose this happened to your wife today."

Looking somber, Kittery nodded, and then whispered, "OK."

Warming to his personal re-enactment of the 'whodunit scene' at the end of an old mystery story, Barn continued, "Maybe your daughter, or someone claiming to be her, came in here with a story about you that's so hot, Payton Place couldn't handle it. What would your wife do?"

"Rip my balls off...sorry...rip my ass off," Kittery answered.

With his dark eyes boring intently into the sergeant's cool, green ones, Barn asked, "Are you sure she wouldn't kill the woman herself?"

Kittery looked at his wife. She was the best woman, probably the best person, he had ever met; in her clear brown eyes, he thought he saw the answer.

"Marge is no killer…she'd have come to me," he answered decisively.

Barn looked quizzically at Marge; even as he opened his mouth to speak, he knew his question was a loaded one.

"Would you?" he asked.

The white-haired woman looked at the blond girl seated at her table. To no one's shock more than her husband's, she answered, "If I'd had the axe in my hands right at the exact minute she told me, I think I might've done it, but never after having a chance to think it over…a chance to talk to Mitch."

She took a sip of coffee, as though washing away the taste of the painful admission, and finished, "I couldn't have done it a day later. I'd have told Mitch to take care of it."

As the scenario untangled itself in his mind, Mitch looked at Barn, and asked, "So you think she put him up to killing Gloria Baines?"

"Not necessarily killing her," Barn answered. "I think she told Whit about it, not dreaming he'd kill her, but just hoping he'd talk to her, report her to Russ Johnson, if he had to…but make her go away. I doubt she'd have seen him as a potential killer, but the man had every bit as much to lose."

"How so?" Kittery asked. "You mean because he'd lose his home? You're forgetting…even if she sold the property for what would amount to chump change…"

Passionately, Barn cut in, "No, it's not just about the money for Gretchen…there's a principle here. This is the only home she's ever had."

"So she goes to her husband, and tells him to do something… or else?" Kittery conjectured.

"Maybe she said 'or else' maybe not. I don't know," Barn answered. "What I do think is based on the pretty obvious fact that Whit's been living the life of Riley. His wife forgave his shortcomings in the past, and, who knows, she might eventually have let this blow over too…but I bet not if she lost her home."

Arnie interjected, "Right, and the old bastard knew he couldn't chance losing his free pass. Taking it to Russ Johnson was just gonna mean one more person knew about it. It would end up in the paper probably, and eventually, Gretchen might be embarrassed enough to kick him out on his ass."

Giving his partner a glance across the table, he added, "Neither one of us think she believed he'd be capable of this, but I'm willing to bet it's all she's thought of since

Russ Johnson went over there yesterday morning to find out if they were missing an axe."

Mitch contemplated all the junior detectives had told him, and then said, "Well, boys, that's a nice, neat little theory, but for one detail. What about the note?" Smiling good-naturedly at them, he said, "Crime solving isn't easy."

In truth, he was sorry to shoot a hole in their theory—it was pretty good.

Barn laughed, "Shit, I forgot this part, and it's the clincher; I don't know where my mind went."

Relishing the theatrics, he tied the bow on the gift of his theory by telling the little group at the kitchen table what he had remembered last night.

"Gretchen told us, and, again, this was on the first night we met her, that George Parker used to beat his wife; she said Bessie gave her a key, and she'd sneak in after the lights were out, and, uh, make sure Bessie wasn't dead on the floor."

With a flourish, he added, "She told us she still has the key; George never knew she had it…no one did…no one except Whit."

Mitch Kittery sat back in his chair, impressed at the way the two young men had woven the circumstantial evidence together; if they were right, Whit Grissom could very easily have taken the key far into the night, written out the note and delivered it. 'Barney' was the name he had chosen to sign by simple chance.

It did not take Einstein Jr. to figure out that, if Gretchen gossiped about Whit to everyone else, she very likely gossiped about everyone else to Whit. If the old woman knew the names of guests at the inn at any given time, it was a safe bet that Whit did too.

Kittery sighed, and said, "I think I'll give Russ Johnson a call; the two of us need to pay a little visit on the Grissoms.

Chapter 25

The old codgers did not show up quite this early.

Hearing the tinkling of the brass bell over the door, the old woman moved from the tavern's kitchen out into the main room, where she found two men standing on the drinking side of the bar; she was not surprised to see at least one of them.

Kittery had no obligation to call Russ, and certainly was not obliged to tell him exactly how he had come into possession of the knowledge he had, but he had done so. He liked the man, and also sensed he would be a calming influence in what had the potential to be a volatile scene.

"Been expecting you back, Russ," Gretchen said, a resigned tone in her voice. "I knew the stupid old bastard screwed himself with that cockamamie story about a big axe."

She looked relieved; she had been carrying too heavy a burden for too long a time—24 hours felt like 24 years.

Looking directly into the bartender's eyes, the state trooper could see only grief and resignation, where there once had been joie de vivre. Russ asked the question he supposed he had known the answer to in his heart since yesterday morning, "There was no such axe, was there?"

Gretchen smiled, tears beginning to well up in her sad eyes, "Course not...it's George Parker's axe you'll be looking for; I have no idea what's become of it..."

Mitch interrupted, "Mrs. Grissom, I'm Sergeant Mitch Kittery from the State Police."

"Yes, sir," Gretchen answered promptly. "I saw your people around yesterday." Looking back at Russ, with whom she felt more comfortable, she said in a rush, "I didn't know he'd do a thing like this, Russ...I didn't wanna lose my home; it's all I have. Gloria's his daughter; neither of us ever knew about her."

Either of the two law enforcement officers could have stopped her there, but both had the same instinct—let her tell the entire story in her own way; questions would come later.

Gretchen continued, "She told me that night she'd keep her mouth shut, if I'd sell her the tavern for what it's really worth." The old woman seemed, for a moment, about to crumble. Tears filled her eyes, and spilled down her weathered cheeks. Hands rising to wipe away the most visible signs of her emotion, she continued in a steady voice, "She said something about wanting to sell it to those same developer people who've been calling me."

The old woman interrupted her narrative for only as long as it took her to pull a tissue from the end of her sleeve and blow her nose.

Still silent, the men listened as she detailed the events of the night before Gloria's murder.

"I told her to get out. I said I needed time to think. She left somewhere around ten o'clock, and I closed up right away…my blood was boiling. Whit went outside with his cronies, saying goodnight like always, I suppose, and went up the outside stairs."

Her blood must have been boiling then, too, for she pulled off a draft for herself, and took a long swig before continuing, "I flung the upstairs door back so hard, the damned knob put a hole in the wall. He was already sitting down, but he jumped up damned fast when I started screaming at him. We had a real battle—just words, Whit's never been violent—but the man can cuss, and so can I when I'm mad enough."

She thumped the beer mug down on the bar, heedless of the golden liquid that splattered over the rim. Her eyes flashed with fury as she looked from one man to the other and said, "I wanted to put a hole in the old bastard…if he was dead right now, I'd be the one who did it."

Drawing in a calming breath, she continued, "I told the old bastard to get rid of her, and I gave him what money I had. I said to him, 'Whit, I don't care how much more it takes, just give her this, and tell her to go away…we'll pay her off. I just can't lose my place…it's all I got'."

She wiped her eyes again, and finished, "I even told him I'd forgive him, if he'd just do this, and save our place…I meant give her the money. I swear I didn't mean kill her…" Open sobs prevented her from saying more.

Looking at the woman behind the bar, Kittery understood that the suspicions of his young visitors that morning hit very close to dead center on the target. The tavern was a priceless treasure to Gretchen—it was her home.

Whit treasured it too, but for a far different reason. His wife and her tavern were like frequent flyer miles, and he was using both of them for a free ride through life.

From what Gretchen Grissom was telling them, her first thought was not for the police either, and Mitch smiled mentally to himself. Someday, he would tell his daughter about that; it would make her feel less of a fool.

Mitch saw just one thing in a slightly different light than his morning visitors had. Although the end result was probably the same, Whit wasn't worrying only that his wife might eventually throw him out. He was worrying that she might forgive him, but pay everything she had for Gloria Baines' silence—he had to do something before she gave away good money.

Russ seated himself before the proprietress, and reached across the bar to take one of her hands.

"Gretchen" he began, "Gloria's not Whit's illegitimate daughter, it was a scam...she worked for the developer's attorney."

Glancing quickly sideways at his colleague, he added, "Lizzie Tidman was in a fix financially too, that's how she got roped up in this...she tried to stop it."

"Not hard enough," Gretchen retorted through her tears, her voice accusatory.

His voice growing more gentle, Russ quietly explained, "Lizzie didn't do anything wrong, Gretchen; she's Sergeant Kittery's daughter, in fact, and this morning, she told her dad all about Gloria's plan. She's been like you, Gretchen...too scared to talk right away."

Watching the trooper in action, Mitch Kittery liked what he saw. Immediately appealing to the fears that had kept the old woman silent for a full day, the slightly younger man made her realize that Lizzie had been paddling the same canoe.

Taking over the interview with a nod to his temporary partner, Mitch asked, "Where's your husband ma'am? We've gotta talk to him."

She smiled sadly, "In the bedroom...lazy bastard's still asleep."

Pointing toward the door behind the bar, she said, "Just go through the kitchen, and around that big cabinet; the stairs are behind it. Let me lock the tavern door, and I'll be right up there. Wait at the top for me…door's locked."

As she rounded the bar and then went over to bolt the tavern door, she continued speaking to the man she had known almost since God put him on the earth. "Russ, I know I should've told you right away, but I just couldn't do it…"

"Tell me what you know, Gretchen. We'll talk to the sergeant about it together."

Standing with her back against the tavern door, hands on her hips, she explained, "He wrote a note the night before, telling her to meet him outside in the morning, and he snuck over with it around midnight…"

"That would be the note he signed 'Barney'," Russ said.

"He didn't!" Gretchen said, amazed.

Mopping her face with her hands, she said, "Dear God, I can't believe he tried to link that nice boy to this."

She shook her head again, and continued, "When he got back here yesterday morning, after, I thought, going to talk to her and give her the money, he was as white as a ghost. I begged him to tell me what he'd done, and he finally did…"

"He planned to kill her, then," Russ cut in.

"I guess he did," Gretchen answered in a bone-weary voice. "He probably would've taken our axe, except that on his way out of the inn during the night, he told me that he noticed the moon glinting off of something by the garbage cans, and realized that George Parker had left his axe out there. When he went back, he just took the axe, and waited around the corner of the house until he saw Gloria come outside…all he had to do then was sneak up behind her."

"Not quite all," Russ answered. "He had to take one powerful swing…I'm surprised the effort didn't kill him."

Epilogue

Barn sprawled comfortably on the firm cushions of the new, high-backed sofa bed in the den, his tiny, sock-covered feet pointing toward the window.

Fluffy snowflakes nearly the size of his fist drifted lazily down to the ground, the day's chill wind occasionally swirling them along in lacy, whirlpool patterns.

At the opposite end of the den, Arnie Kotkin hunched over his desk, a load of books and sheaves of loose papers spread out before him as he crammed for midterms.

As the afternoon crawled along toward evening and snow continued to fall, Barn said, "Arnie, this is the second consecutive year we've ended thinking about killings."

Without raising his strained, hazel eyes from the books, Arnie answered, "I hadn't been thinking of this one, Barn; thanks for mentioning it."

"No trouble."

Arnie looked up, and studied the back of the sofa bed at the other end of the room; behind its high, well-stuffed back, his tiny partner was invisible.

From his place at the desk, Arnie could see over the lower back of their old sofa bed; he did miss being able to watch Barn nap on the sofa in the evenings, as he sometimes did.

As the studying student observed, "At least my brother's killer was brought to justice," he had the odd sensation that he was speaking to their furniture.

"So was Gloria's," Barn answered drolly. "Whit just happened to answer to a higher authority."

"I doubt the Almighty dispensed of Whit with a massive heart attack the night before Mitch Kittery showed up to arrest him…" Arnie began, refusing to believe that God got him.

"You're kidding, right?" Barn queried, sitting up, and poking his nose over the top of the couch. "The old bastard dies of a heart attack in his sleep the night after he chops someone's head off, and you think God had nothing to do with it? What happened to 'Vengeance is mine sayeth the Lord'?"

Arnie answered simply, "I prefer to think of a gentler God—not one who nails unsuspecting people in their sleep." He lowered his eyes back to his work.

"It's not like it was an unsuspecting innocent person, Arnie," Barn said. "It was Whit Grissom. God could see He needed to, um, smite him, and He did."

The student valiantly trying to study for his tests looked up again. "All right" he said, "I'll accept that God helped things fall into place for Gretchen…"

In one smooth move Barn was off the couch, and heading for the desk. "You'd believe that God made a huge real estate developer back out of a deal, leaving George Parker so desperate to sell out that he practically gave her the inn, but you can't see that God dispensed with the old bastard to set everything else in motion?" He sounded incredulous.

"God doesn't kill one person to bring good fortune to another," Arnie insisted. "Besides, that would have to mean it was in His plan for Gloria to be murdered too, just to be sure the developer would back out."

"I hadn't considered that point yet," Barn said, a wicked grin spreading across his face. Irreverently, he commented, "It is a bit drastic, even for someone who flooded the entire planet…"

"Watch yourself," Arnie playfully cautioned. "God might just get you…that was nasty."

Barn laughed, and said, "God knows I was kidding. It's true, though. Scripture says, 'The last shall be first, and the first shall be last'. I'll bet Gretchen was never first in her entire life. God rewarded her."

Giving in to the laugh Barn was trying so hard to get, Arnie said, "Blessed be."

About the Author

Susan M. Hooper was employed as a legal secretary/legal assistant for 23 years before hitting the craft circuit as a doll maker in 1996 and beginning to write comedic fan fiction pieces about a year later. Murder Junction is her second novel, and it features some of the characters from her first novel, Belle Harbor Skeletons.

Ms. Hooper resides in Connecticut with her family, which includes members of the four-legged variety as well; specifically three cats and two yellow Labs…so walking is an obvious hobby.

Printed in the United States
23410LVS00003B/160